HIS CONVENIENT MATCH: A REGENCY ROMANCE

LOST FORTUNES, FOUND LOVE (BOOK 6)

ROSE PEARSON

HIS CONVENIENT MATCH

PROLOGUE

"*T*homas."

It had been years since someone had called him by his given name. The only person he could ever recall doing so was his mother. Thomas frowned, his eyes still tightly closed.

Is she here?

That would make very little sense. Why would his mother be in London? As far as he knew, she was quite contented back at his estate, having no desire to come to the London Season this year.

"Mother?"

Thomas tried to speak, tried to say his mother's name, but could not seem to do so. His lips felt bruised and his mind was uncooperative. He simply could not fathom where he was, caught somewhere between dreams and awakening, unable to comprehend what this strange reality could be.

"I think he might be close to death."

A man's voice came from very far away and Thomas' heart immediately began to pound furiously. Who was it that was near to dying? Was it one of his friends - and if so, which one?

Something was pressed against his forehead, and Thomas tried to lift a hand to it, but his arm and hand simply would not move. It was extremely disconcerting, being in a body where one could hear and feel a good many things but could not respond in any clear way... and without having a clear reason as to why it was so.

"We should find someone." There was a heavy tone to the second man's voice – and at that point, Thomas realized that he recognized neither of the men's voices. "Something's wrong with this fellow and I don't know what to do to help 'im."

Slowly, Thomas came to the realization that these two people were talking about him. *He* was the one they believed to be near death. A sudden panic sent his heart into a furious rhythm, and his breathing grew quicker, but still, his eyes would not open.

"Did you see that?" There was a slight nudge of excitement in the first man's voice. "Something happened, I think... I think he can hear us."

"You'll be all right, fella!" The second man's voice grew suddenly loud as though he was afraid that Thomas would not hear him if he spoke in a lower tone. "You maybe just had too much of the good stuff. Your head's not quite right."

Still, Thomas tried to speak, but words would not come. Violently demanding that his eyes open, he worked with all of his might to lift the lids and let him see, but nothing changed. A groan of frustration pushed up from his throat, escaping from between his lips, and both men watching him let out a loud exclamation.

"You're coming back," one of them cried, his hand

pushing Thomas' shoulder. "You're coming back to your-self. You maybe need a few more minutes."

"It'll probably take some time, but you're getting there," said the second. "Don't know what would have happened to you if you'd been left here lying by yourself. Don't you have any friends? People round this part are always with their friends. Safer that way."

Despite the questions, Thomas could not answer them, his frustration growing - combined with a small flicker of fear that he would never be able to open his eyes or speak a single word again.

"I'll stay with you," the second man continued, perhaps able to see the agonized expression he was sure now spread itself across his face, or mayhap guessing at all of the fear which was currently in his thoughts. "We won't go and leave you. However long it takes, we'll stay."

"We're just hopeful for a coin or two for the trouble," the second man continued, a slight chuckle in his voice. "Don't you worry now. You'll come back to yourself soon enough. You just need to wait."

"Gentlemen?" A voice – a different voice, quieter, softer, and altogether more feminine, reached Thomas' ears. "Oh, thank goodness you have found him!"

Something soft and warm pressed to his cheek, a gentle breath running across his skin.

"I will take care of you."

"You know this gentleman?"

One of the original men sounded a little disappointed, but as Thomas tried to speak, the new voice came again.

"Yes, I do. His carriage is waiting. Please, help me take him. I will pay you handsomely for the trouble."

The pain in Thomas' head grew as the two men came to shift him bodily. He tried not to give in to the encroaching darkness – but it was much too difficult. The pain of being moved seemed to send fresh agonies to his head and, after a moment, he welcomed the darkness. It was all he had.

∾

"AND THAT IS when I awoke. Lord Wiltsham's arrival brought me here thereafter." Thomas shifted in his seat and spread out his hands, settling his arms on his knees as he sat forward. Every movement was considered and careful as if proving to himself that he was, in fact, able to move freely rather than being forced to lie flat out on the cold stone floor. Taking a breath, Thomas looked around the room. "I have no recollection of anything other than that."

Every face in the room was solemn, each of them contemplating the reality of what had happened, and realizing slowly just how much this was to change their futures.

"We have all been tricked; all taken in." Lord Stoneleigh, white-faced and in pain, grimaced. "It is no coincidence that we all lost some significant amount of coin last evening."

"Significant?" Lord Foster shook his head. "I have lost almost everything."

"As have I." Muttering, Thomas put his head in his hands. "And what is worse, I cannot remember a single thing. I do not even recall walking into that gambling den last evening. I do not remember signing a letter requiring that my entire fortune be sent to another's account – an account which has now been emptied, evidently." Drawing air into his lungs, he let it out again slowly. "You are quite certain that we were all there last evening, Foster?"

"Yes." Lord Foster's white face looked back at him "Yes, we were all present with Lord Gillespie. He was the one who told us where to go, the one who led us in that direction."

"But he is acquainted with all of us and a close friend to some," Lord Wiltsham put in. "Surely he cannot have done anything untoward? He would not injure us so."

"Perhaps, perhaps not." Lord Foster's eyes grew dark. "At this moment I know nothing. I am lost."

"We are all lost." Thomas rubbed one hand across his forehead, gritting his teeth against the dull ache which had settled there some hours ago, sensing it growing. "Why is it that I can remember nothing? It does not make any sense."

"None of this makes sense." Lord Thornbridge placed one hand against his forehead, heaving a heavy sigh as he mimicked Thomas' gesture. "The question remains, however, what is it that we are to do?"

Nobody could give any answer, and Thomas found his spirit growing suddenly dark. What could be done? He could not remember anything about last evening, aside from the fact that he had found himself on a cold, dark stone floor and had, thereafter, been taken from there by another. When his consciousness had returned, he had woken up in his own rooms, confused and unsure about all that had taken place.

And then a note had arrived from Lord Wiltsham.

"There is nothing to be done." His heart sinking ever lower, Thomas closed his eyes, leaned forward, pushed his hands through his hair, and settled his elbows on his knees. "You must face the truth. We must face *reality* – and the reality is that there is nothing to be done. We are now impoverished men. *I* am a destitute gentleman and, it seems, shall ever more be so."

CHAPTER ONE

"Where are you to go?"

Thomas snorted.

"Where else am I to go but to White's? It is the only place that I can drown my sorrows."

Lord Thornbridge dropped one hand on Thomas' shoulder.

"Do not be too despondent. I am certain that all will be well. We will find a way."

"And yet I do not have your confidence." Thomas spoke brusquely, having no interest in Lord Thornbridge's encouragements. "You are just as despondent as I, I am sure. You seem determined to make the best of it, but I am not so easily convinced. In fact, I am afraid that I have already given in."

Lord Thornbridge frowned.

"Given in to what?"

"To despair." Thomas spoke honestly, shrugging. "I can remember nothing. Not a single moment of last evening is still in my mind. I am aware that some of you recall a little more, but that will do *me* no good."

Lord Thornbridge opened his mouth, clearly intending to say something more, but then shut it again with a snap, turning his head away. There was a bleakness in his face, matching that which Thomas felt heavy upon his own heart, a darkness that could not be escaped. Some of his friends might try to find hope, encouragement, and strength where they could, but Thomas would not. He was determined to be sober-minded, to face the situation with honesty. Yes, it was dark and desperate, but he would face it, nonetheless.

"I suppose White's will not want our patronage any longer, once news of our poverty is known."

Lord Thornbridge shot his friend a dark smile.

"I believe you are right."

"Therefore, it seems as though my plan is a thorough one, for what opportunity will I have to drink fine whiskey and excellent brandy in the next few years?"

Lord Thornbridge held his gaze steadily for some moments. Then, with a dry laugh, shook his head.

"You mean to get foxed?"

Thomas shrugged again, caring very little for what Lord Thornbridge thought of him, given the circumstances, then nodded.

"And I shall enjoy every mouthful."

"And thereafter?"

Taking in a deep breath, Thomas let it out in a sigh.

"Thereafter, I think I intend to turn tail and hide at my estate. I will, I am sure, have to go through my finances very carefully indeed, and will be required to make a great many changes. But for now, I intend to enjoy one last evening in London society, where I am still seen as a respectable fellow and not one who has lost his fortune in a foolish night of gambling."

"Lord Foster is sure that –"

Thomas held up one hand, palm out, towards his friend.

"Pray do not try to encourage me to think differently about the matter. It will not work. My mind is made up."

Grimacing, Lord Thornbridge nodded but looked away. With a scowl, Thomas turned on his heel and immediately began to make his way for the door, having every intention of going directly to White's.

"You are leaving now?"

Glancing over his shoulder, Thomas nodded.

"What else is there to do, Lord Thornbridge?"

"But it is only a little past noon. You cannot intend to spend the rest of the day and night there, surely?"

A hard smile settled over Thomas' face.

"I can see nothing else worth doing to fill my time, can you? I have no hope. I have no future here. My time in London society as an honorable, respectable, wealthy gentleman has come to an end, and the only thing I can think to do is drink to that."

~

"ANOTHER."

Well aware that he was building up a heavy debt in White's, Thomas grinned when Lord Thornbridge sent him another look.

"I will be gone from London, remember? What difference do my actions here make?"

"What of your honor? You are always a gentleman who pays his debts. Do not become one who does not do so, especially when you are without funds."

"If you would not mind, I would prefer it if you kept your voice low." Speaking with great dignity, Thomas rolled his eyes at his friend, already half cut. "You may be perfectly contented that the *ton* know at this immediate moment that we are no longer wealthy gentlemen but I, myself, am not."

"The truth will come out." Lord Thornbridge waved away the footman, refusing another drink. Clearly, he had decided that he was not going to partake as heavily as Thomas. "There is no escaping that."

"But it can stay far from me for a short while. At least until tomorrow!" Holding up his glass to Lord Thornbridge, Thomas shot a hard smile toward his friend. "You would not want to spoil this evening for me, now would you?"

With a sigh, Lord Thornbridge pushed himself out of his chair.

"No, I certainly would not, but nor do I wish to stay here and watch you drink yourself into oblivion."

"What?" Thomas lifted his eyebrows high. "Are you truly going to leave me here alone?"

Lord Thornbridge rolled his eyes and folded his arms across his chest.

"It is not as though you are here alone!" He gestured to the large crowd that was now in White's. They had been here for some hours, and still, Thomas was not ready to leave, but it was clear that Lord Thornbridge was no longer desirous of the company here. "Pray forgive me, but I still must take my leave of you, Silverton."

Thomas' eyebrows dropped.

"Do as you must."

With eyes that were slightly heavy, he followed Lord Thornbridge as he walked from White's. Yes, he had shrugged nonchalantly and yes, he had told Lord Thornbridge to do as he pleased, but the truth was that he would have preferred his friend's company. Picking up his brandy, he threw it back and then slammed the glass down hard on the table. Lifting his hand, he waved to catch the footman's attention so that he might order another, only for another fellow to come and sit down beside him.

"We shall drink them out of all the brandy they have," he chortled, as Thomas barely managed to raise a smile, not quite sure that he wanted company – especially company he could not recall the name of.

"I hardly think that will be the case." With slightly curved lips, Thomas tried to catch the footman's attention again, but the man was turning to serve another gentleman. "I will not be able to get another drink, given that the footmen here seem to be eager to ignore me."

"Allow me to be of aid to you."

Raising his hand, the gentleman managed to catch the footman's attention in an instant. Thomas did not allow the flicker of irritation to delve further into his heart, rather finding himself somewhat satisfied when the other gentleman ordered two brandies for them each and declared that he would pay the bill.

"Are you in something of a despondency?"

His question made Thomas frown.

"I am a little melancholy, that is all"

"Then I am certain that this brandy will lift your spirits a great deal."

Thomas smiled.

"Excellent."

He made no effort to try to recollect the man's name. What would be the point of doing so? He was soon to be gone from London, never to return. He would have no coin to do so. This was to be his last evening of enjoyment even though his heart was very heavy indeed. In coming here, he had hoped that the more he indulged, the better he would feel but, as yet, such a situation had not occurred. Growing a little weary, Thomas sighed and his heart seemed to drag to the floor. This was not the raucous evening that he had hoped for.

Perhaps that is because I have not yet indulged enough.

A genuine grin spread across his face as he accepted the first brandy.

The gentleman whose name he could not recollect lifted his glass.

"To your very good health and the lifting of your spirits."

Still grinning, Thomas clinked his glass with the other, happy to have the very finest brandy to enjoy.

"May it do so," he declared, as the other gentleman laughed. "And may this be the beginning of a very jovial evening indeed."

$\sim$

By the time Thomas opened his eyes, what had been a dark sky had now turned a little brighter. This was now the second evening where he could not recall what had happened, although on this occasion he had entirely himself to blame. The rolling of the carriage made his stomach twist this way and that, and it took a great deal of control not to cast up his accounts.

At least my driver recalled where it was that I wanted to go.

Allowing his bleary eyes to settle on the various countryside scenes as the carriage continued up the road, Thomas had no doubt as to where they were going. He was to return to his estate, just as he had planned. From there, he would consider his situation and, in facing the truth, would allow it to become a part of his life. He would have to take great measures to make certain that he was not entirely ruined, so much so that, from this day forward, his life would never be the same again. A great and heavy darkness flooded over him, and Thomas closed his eyes, considering now that Lord Thornbridge had been correct. Last night's indulgences had not been worth the trouble, for all he was left with now, was a heavy heart and a painful head. He ought to have been a good deal more sober minded, allowing himself time to take in what had occurred, rather than reacting with such foolishness.

But it was too late now. Come the following morning, he would be back at his estate and would have to face everything in its entirety. There was no escape. His money was gone. His life was broken apart into many, many pieces in a way that he did not believe could ever be put together again.

CHAPTER TWO

"Do you think that Lord Silverton will be here this evening?"

Lady Charlotte Everton looked around the room. She had been acquainted with Lord Silverton the previous year - they had found themselves quite warmly acquainted, in fact. There had been nothing of significance, however, for she was only on her first Season, but she *had* found herself eager to be in his company again.

"I do not know, my dear." Her mother smiled and patted her hand as the carriage rumbled towards Lord Hackett's townhouse. "But you need not think only of him. This is your second Season, and many will know that you must now give serious consideration to your future. Many a match is made in a second Season."

"Yes, I know, Mama."

Turning her head, Charlotte allowed herself a small smile as she looked out into the inky darkness. She would not pretend to herself that she had no particular interest in Lord Silverton. He was handsome, amiable, and with an excellent standing that would satisfy both her mother and her father.

That being said, she considered that, if Lord Silverton was not at this ball, then there were certainly a good many other gentlemen who might catch her interest. But for the moment, she was very much hoping that Lord Silverton *would* be present this evening – and that they might dance together.

"I have heard that he has been absent from society these last two weeks." Her father cleared his throat. "It is rather strange. There are three or four gentlemen – respectable fellows – who have taken themselves back to their estates. It is odd to do such a thing so close to the beginning of the Season."

Now a little confused, Charlotte looked at her father, struggling to comprehend.

"You mean to say that there are some gentlemen in society who have simply arrived in London and then turned on their heels and gone back to their estates?"

"Yes, that is precisely what I mean."

"And Lord Silverton was one of these gentlemen?"

"Yes, I believe so. Although I have heard at least one person say that he has returned again." Tutting under his breath, Lord Landon gave a slight shake of his head. "It is all very confusing. I would have thought those gentlemen who are as yet unwed – such as Lord Silverton – would want to take full advantage of the Season."

"Well, if he is returned, then there is nothing to concern ourselves with." Lady Landon reached out to press Charlotte's hand. "But as I have reminded you, you need not fix your gaze solely on Lord Silverton. There are many fine gentlemen sure to be present here this Season. Be open-minded about the possibilities, and it will go well for you."

Charlotte smiled at her mother.

"Thank you, Mama."

"Not at all, my dear. You look quite beautiful this evening and I am certain that you will turn many heads."

The remainder of the carriage journey passed in complete silence and Charlotte did not feel the need to break it. This season could offer her many a decadent evening, spent with excellent gentlemen who would converse, smile, laugh, and dance with her.

I should very much like to dance with Lord Silverton. I confess that I do find him very handsome.

The thought of being in his company again sent all of her emotions into a whirlwind, with waves of anticipation rolling through her. She was hot, then cold, then hot again. Stepping down from the carriage, she smoothed her gown, but her mother fussed her hands away, telling her that she looked quite proper already.

"You are not anxious, are you?"

Charlotte laughed, but it brought a tightness to her chest.

"I am a little nervous about reentering society, Mama."

Or is it the hope of seeing Lord Silverton?

Walking into the townhouse a little behind her mother and father, Charlotte kept her eyes forward, rather than looking to the right or left. There were greetings and thanks to be given to their host and, thereafter, the family were ushered into the ballroom. The noise was quite intense, and Charlotte realized that she had quite forgotten just how overwhelming such an event could be.

"Charlotte!"

A loud exclamation came to her left, and Charlotte turned quickly, only to find her hands grasped by tight fingers. Her smile spread immediately.

"Florence! I am so very glad to see you again." Embracing her friend, she laughed as they stood together. "And now, this is our second Season. Can you believe it?"

"I can indeed, for it is all that my mother has been speaking about these last few months." Laughing. Florence took Charlotte's arm and began to promenade around the ballroom, leaving Charlotte's mother to choose whether or not she would fall into step behind them or allow them a few minutes of privacy. To Charlotte's relief, her mother chose the latter, and she allowed herself to let out a deep, long breath which made Lady Florence's eyebrows lift in surprise. "It seems as though I am not the only one who has been a little overwhelmed by their mother!"

Laughing, Charlotte reached across to press her friend's hands.

"My mother has been making me aware that the second Season is when I am expected to make a match."

"And is that something that you hope to do?"

"I do not see why I should not." Charlotte shrugged one shoulder, having barely considered the question for herself. Was this what she wanted? Was this what she *truly* desired for herself? Or had she secretly been pining for another year of freedom? "It is what is expected, and I suppose, therefore, it is something which I have never given much thought to."

"But what if you marry a gentleman for whom you have no feelings?" Lady Florence turned to look into Charlotte's face. "What happens then?"

The question made very little sense to her.

"I do not think that anything happens other than I continue with my life as a married lady and do everything I can to be a suitable wife and mistress of his house. When the time comes, I raise his children and make certain that they are brought up in much the same way that I myself was, so that they are suitable young ladies and gentlemen." Lady Florence shook her head, clearly distressed by Charlotte's remarks with her lips tightening. "You do not agree with me then?"

Letting go of Charlotte's arm, Lady Florence threw up both of her hands.

"How could you even ask me such a thing? We have been friends for some time, and I am *certain* that I have told you about my dreams of love and affection between myself and my husband." Her eyes narrowed a little. "Pray tell me that you do not think me ridiculous for having such notions as this. My mother already thinks me quite ridiculous, and I would find myself deeply upset if you also believed me to be so."

Charlotte shook her head quickly.

"No, not in the least. I suppose it is not something that I have ever given much consideration to, but I would not ever call you ridiculous or foolish."

Lady Florence settled both hands on her waist, tilted her head and studied Charlotte as though suspicious that Charlotte was deliberately hiding something from her. Not certain as to what this could be, Charlotte looked back at her friend, calmly waiting for Lady Florence to express her next question, which she was sure would come very soon.

"Tell me, you have an interest in Lord Silverton, do you not?"

"In Lord Silverton?" Attempting to laugh, Charlotte shook her head and turned her face away. "I think him a fine gentleman, but London is full of amiable gentlemen."

"Aha!" Leaning forward Lady Florence patted Charlotte on the arm lightly. "I knew I was right! You *do* consider Lord Silverton to be of particular interest!"

"I have never said such a thing."

The heat which rose in her face embarrassed her so much that Charlotte continued to look away from her friend. Unfortunately, her high color only made Lady Florence laugh all the more.

"You need not pretend." Coming to stand beside Charlotte again, Lady Florence looped her hand through her arm. "It is quite all right to notice such gentlemen. You need not admit it to me, but it is something I am clearly now well aware of."

"I do not understand your reasons for asking me such a thing."

Still a little flushed, Charlotte tried to grimace at her friend, only for Lady Florence to chuckle.

"I ask you because I am trying to prove my point." she continued, merrily. "Tell me this: if you had to choose between two gentlemen, with one being a fellow who you had no interest in, nor feelings for whatsoever, and the other being someone such as Lord Silverton, who you have some interest in, then which gentleman would you prefer to wed?"

"That is no question at all." Unfortunately for Charlotte, the warmth in her face continued to grow as her friend looked at her steadily, waiting for her reply. There was no doubt in Charlotte's mind at all that, when it came to Lord Silverton, the choice between him and another fellow would be no choice at all. She would immediately be drawn to Lord Silverton. "I do not think that I shall ever be in that situation, so the question is moot."

"Indulge me." Lady Florence's eyes twinkled. "Truly, there cannot be anything to say that you would hide from me, given that we are such *excellent* friends."

Charlotte blinked, all too aware that the answer was no

doubt already in her eyes. There seemed nothing for her to do but to be honest. A sigh emitted from her lips as she rolled her eyes.

"Very well, if you must know, then yes, I should prefer Lord Silverton."

She spoke with as much dignity as she could manage, but Lady Florence only giggled and squeezed her arm.

"You see?" Putting her head a little closer to Charlotte's so that they might speak in private, Lady Florence spoke in a lower tone. "There is much to be said for feelings of the heart. Do not allow anyone to tell you otherwise."

Charlotte considered this as they continued to promenade slowly around the ballroom. The truth was that no one had ever dissuaded her from allowing affection to be a part of her considerations. Rather, it was not an idea that she had ever indulged. Her parents both appeared very contented indeed, and theirs had been a practical match. Her mother had told her often of it and thus that was all Charlotte had ever considered for herself.

"I have heard that Lord Silverton has been absent from society of late." Charlotte murmured half to herself as she caught Lady Florence's surprised glance. "My father has informed me of it."

A slight frown drew Lady Florence's eyebrows together.

"I have heard of a few gentlemen who have been in London and then removed themselves from here, but I did not know that Lord Silverton was one of them... although that is most likely because I was not paying any attention to him whatsoever."

She giggled at this, and Charlotte allowed herself a small smile, knowing full well that Lady Florence had no interest in Lord Silverton because she was intrigued by another gentleman.

"And just how is Lord Kirkwood? Has he returned to Scotland as yet? Or will he stay in London a little longer?"

Lady Florence laughed softly, her eyes bright.

"I have given him a reason to stay."

Charlotte's eyebrows lifted.

"Is that so? And shall there soon be news of a particular arrangement between you?"

Lady Florence squeezed Charlotte's arm.

"We are now courting."

Charlotte stopped walking at once, only for Lady Florence to sigh with evident happiness. Her eyes were shining and there was a smile on her face that Charlotte had never seen before, a smile which could only speak of one thing – an emotion that Charlotte herself had never experienced.

"Goodness, how wonderful! I am truly glad for you. I would ask if you are happy, but I can already see from your smile that you *are* so. I do not think I have ever seen you look so joyous."

Lady Florence's smile grew even brighter than Charlotte had ever thought possible.

"That is because my heart is happy." Lady Florence's voice had grown a little softer. "This is what happens when you find yourself courted by a gentleman whom you *truly* have an interest in, who engages your heart. I would encourage you to think about what your heart desires rather than settling on a gentleman you are certain would suit you well enough."

Charlotte could not think of what to say, looking at her friend in pure astonishment. Yes, they were well acquainted, but this was a new honesty that she had never before experienced from Lady Florence. Her throat was a little dry as she tried to summon some response and all the while, Lady Florence only smiled.

"I – I shall consider it."

"Good. I –"

Her friend stopped, her gaze fixing to something over Charlotte's shoulder. Lady Florence caught her breath and then smiled – and immediately, something twisted hard in Charlotte's stomach. Daring a glance, she looked over her shoulder. Her breath quickened, and without realizing she was doing it, one hand went to her stomach.

Lord Silverton had arrived.

CHAPTER THREE

This was not wise.

"You did not need to come."

Thomas jerked slightly, having quite forgotten that he was standing close to Lord Thornbridge.

"Yes, I did." He realized that he was scowling, and it took Thomas a moment to remove the expression from his features. "It has been some weeks since I was in society and, since then, you have all written to me to tell me of your success in regaining your fortunes. It would be foolish of me to stay away, even though I am quite certain that I shall not have the same success."

"Why should you say such a thing?" Lord Thornbridge smiled and lifted a hand to someone before turning his attention back towards Thomas. "If the five of us have managed to regain our fortunes, then there can be no difficulty with you, surely. You must now have some hope, at the very least!"

Thomas shook his head, seeing Lord Thornbridge's eyes flare.

"There is a reason for that, of course," he continued

before his friend could protest. "You all recalled some detail, some fact about what had taken place. I have not even a single moment of knowledge. I cannot remember even the smallest thing. That is to my disadvantage, and *that* is why I believe that I will ultimately fail."

Lord Thornbridge muttered something, but Thomas could not make it out. Keeping his rather severe expression fixed in place, he turned his head away, looking around the room, and finding his heart sinking heavily. The last few weeks back at his estate had been very difficult, as he had fought to find a way to face his future without giving in to despair. Now that he was back in London, however, it was almost torturous knowing that, no doubt, the *ton* would surely be aware by now of his current poverty. Very few people would wish to be near him. The friends whom he'd once had, he would no longer be able to call friend, they would not even be acquaintances! He would be rejected and, unless he could find a way to recover his fortune, would be pushed away entirely. Silently preparing himself for all that would come with this evening, he found himself blowing out a long, slow breath.

"You need not look so anxious." Lord Thornbridge's rumble caught through Thomas' thoughts. "I have heard none speaking of you these last few days"

"That is a small comfort at least." Taking a deep breath, he tried to smile, but failed spectacularly, catching the frown which grew across Lord Thornbridge's forehead. "I am well aware that I do not seem amiable but that, I suppose, does not particularly matter, given my present circumstances. I am no longer seeking a bride. None will be able to pull me towards the altar. In time, I shall be pushed away from society and thereafter, forced to live my life entirely alone. This is my one last hope, and it is a hope that I feel already fading."

"Then pray do not allow despondency to take hold of you." Lord Thornbridge's voice was firm, as though he were telling a small child what was expected of him. "You need not give in to fear."

"It is not fear," Thomas retorted, a little sharply. "I am not afraid, merely accepting. I *accept* my situation as it is at present, including all of the struggles and difficulties which come with it."

"But surely you can see that you need not do so." Lord Thornbridge's voice was a little deeper now. "There *is* hope." Thomas made to answer but was suddenly distracted by a face in the crowd - a face that he recognized. A face that had once been of interest to him, but which, now, he considered to be someone he had to quickly forget. So resolved, he turned his head sharply away and did not see how Lady Charlotte's smile faded. "If you can, do try to keep a cheery disposition." Lord Thornbridge's voice was heavy. "We are doing what we can to place you back in society for now – and since no one has spoken of your situation at present, perhaps it is that your plight is still hidden."

"I hardly think so."

Lord Thornbridge's sigh brought nothing but frustration to Thomas. Did the man not realize that he was in such a dire situation that there appeared to be no way out? The moment he began to speak with other members of the *ton,* they would be ready to listen to every word he had to say before, no doubt reporting it back as gossip to their many eager listeners. Every detail of his life – his impoverished life – would be shared with as many of the *ton* as had ears.

"You will scare away all of the lovely young ladies."

Seeming to mutter to himself, Lord Thornbridge turned

on his heel, leaving Thomas to follow him. Thomas did not find himself willing to go after Lord Thornbridge, however. Instead, his gaze turned back to where he had seen Lady Charlotte only a few moments ago. His disappointment at not spying her there any longer was practically palpable and he glanced about, a little embarrassed, as though others around him would be able to feel his sudden frustration and the sharp pain that ran through him.

I cannot draw close to her.

Muttering to himself, Thomas passed one hand over his eyes, quickly trying to shield out the sight of the lovely Lady Charlotte. Last Season, they had become rather friendly, to the point that he considered her a charming young lady. Good breeding, excellent character, and a laugh that always made him smile. Now, however, she was going to have to be set aside, just as every other young lady in London would have to be.

"Since it seems that you will not seem to come to speak to me, I thought I should come to speak with you."

Thomas turned his head towards where Lady Charlotte was now standing, astonished to see her directly in front of him. He had turned his head away so firmly that he had not seen her approach him. Now that she was nearby, however, he had no other choice but to answer her.

"I - I am certain that I would have made my way towards you in time, Lady Charlotte."

Her eyebrow lifted.

"In time?"

His response seemed to astonish her, for her eyes widened and a slight pink came to her cheeks. Thomas could not blame her. Usually, she was one of the first people he spoke with whenever he entered a room where she was present. Now, however, it must appear as though he was doing his best to push her away, to remind her that she was only an acquaintance and nothing more.

But that is as it must be. No doubt she will know the truth about my circumstances sooner or later. Perhaps her mother or father have decided not to tell her the truth about my situation, given that I was away from London. Now that I have returned, however, I am certain it will be whispered into her ear soon enough.

Lady Charlotte continued blinking for some moments before she turned her head away, her lips thin and tight rather than in their full blossom. Her face had colored a little more, and one glance at her hands told him that she was clenching and unclenching them into tight fists, obviously eager to control her emotions and keep a calm façade... something he considered that she was doing very well indeed.

"That is a little unexpected from you, Lord Silverton." Thomas' heart began to tear. It was not as though he had ever had a great depth of feeling for Lady Charlotte, but she *had* been of interest to him, at least. Regardless of whether she was only an acquaintance, or something more, he did not like injuring her so. That was not the sort of gentleman he purported to be and to see her so obviously confused was upsetting to him. And yet he had no other choice. "You have been away from London I understand."

"Yes."

He said nothing more, seeing her eyes narrow slightly. There was no need to indulge her with any further explanation. It would be shameful to him to have to speak of it, and yet it was something that he knew would be told to her very soon, no doubt. He did not want her to hear it from his own lips, however. He had too much pride for that.

Lady Charlotte smiled, but it was gone in an instant.

Her eyes were sparkling, but not with any sort of delight, and that awareness caused a coldness to run over his skin, sending goosebumps up his arms. Her fair golden curls fell lightly about her forehead, and cascaded down her back from a knot high on her head, bringing light to her expression - but her smile was not one which lingered. She was just as beautiful as he had ever considered her, but the ice in her expression pierced his heart.

"It seems as though our conversation has become rather stilted, Lord Silverton." Lady Charlotte lifted her chin, holding his gaze. "I should not like to trouble you if there are others here this evening whom you would prefer to speak to, instead of myself."

Thomas wanted to shake his head and say that he was sorry but instead forced himself to nod.

"Perhaps that would be for the best, Lady Charlotte."

Her eyes flared and then snapped shut for a moment. She swallowed, opened her eyes, and, without another word, turned on her heel and marched away. It was only a few steps towards where her friend was waiting, with her mother a short distance behind, but her displeasure was evident in every step she took. Thomas' gaze begged to linger, but he did not permit it. Instead, he turned around and walked directly across the ballroom, turning himself away from Lady Charlotte and directly towards Lord Thornbridge.

His friend smiled, in antithesis to Thomas' frustration and upset.

"Thus far, I have heard no one mention your present difficulties." Handing him a glass of brandy, Lord Thornbridge's eyebrows lifted. "As I have already suggested, perhaps no one is aware of it as yet."

"That is not very likely," Thomas snorted.

"How can you be so sure?" Lord Thornbridge lifted one eyebrow, but Thomas only shook his head, aware of the shame that began to rattle through him. "Come now. There must be a reason."

Sighing, Thomas looked away.

"Because I believe that I have told the *ton* of my circumstances myself."

There was a slight hitch in Lord Thornbridge's breath and Thomas winced.

"No doubt you will ask me what I mean, and I may as well tell you. You were quite correct."

Lord Thornbridge cleared his throat.

"I – I do not understand. What was I correct about?"

Surprise filled Lord Thornbridge's voice, and Thomas grimaced. He had already experienced enough embarrassment and now was about to shame himself still further by explaining the great mistakes which he had made in not listening to his friend.

"The evening I was determined to become rather foxed – the time I spent in White's. That was the evening when you advised me not to do as I intended."

"Yes, that is so." Lord Thornbridge's frown grew heavier. "But you wrote to me in the days thereafter, stating that you had returned to your estate without difficulty. I assumed that everything was quite–"

"I was very foolish." Rubbing one hand over his eyebrows, Thomas dropped his hand and grimaced. "I do not recall a great deal, but I am quite sure that I would have spoken to those present in White's without hesitation or delay. In my experience, I am often a little loose of the tongue when I have drunk too much. Even though the situation was greatly troubling, and my circumstances dire, I have no doubt that I spoke openly to everyone."

Lord Thornbridge rubbed one hand over his chin, looking hard at Thomas. After some moments, he shook his head.

"No. That does not mean that you said anything. That is only your concern. You have no proof!"

"I would be less inclined to believe that I stayed silent." Dropping his head, Thomas struggled to look back at his friend, such was his embarrassment. "I should have listened to you. It was not a good idea for me to indulge in such a way after such dreadful news. I ought to have remained level-headed. Instead, I am sure that I have brought about my own demise, in terms of my social standing."

Blowing out a breath, Lord Thornbridge handed Thomas another brandy.

"The *ton* is a fickle creature. You know how much they love rumor and whispers. It may be some time before you are fully aware of just how much society knows of your situation, but I would encourage you not to let that fill your mind at present. You are here for one purpose. Fix all of your thoughts on that."

Nodding, Thomas swirled his brandy, then took a small sip. It burned his throat but warmed his chest, chasing away the goosebumps which still lingered from his conversation with Lady Charlotte. His thoughts begged to turn themselves back towards her, but he refused to allow them to, replacing them with ones that concentrated on his present circumstances.

"How is it that I am to try to recall anything?" Taking another quick sip, he glanced around the room. "My mind is completely empty, devoid of anything from that night. I have tried the very best I can to remember anything about what took place, but I cannot even recall sitting at a table with cards in my hand."

Chewing on his lip, he let out a long breath. Perhaps it had been unwise for him to step out this evening. The heaviness was settling upon him all over again, a heaviness that he had thought he could push away by stepping out into society, rather than sitting at home alone. Even if the *ton* rejected him, at least he would have some company by way of Lord Thornbridge and his other acquaintances and friends who were here this evening. Now, however, he felt all the more despondent, reminding himself that he had no knowledge of what had taken place on the night he had lost his fortune. Out of all of his friends, he was the only one who could not remember a single thing. There was no moment where he had felt pain, no flash of memory over seeing some young lady. All there was in his mind was the memory of being in the carriage making its way to the East End and, thereafter, of the following day. The day when he had woken up in a small, cold room and had to be helped to his townhouse by two fellows who had no knowledge of who he was, but had hoped for some recompense for their aid... and the darkness which had come thereafter, when he had realized all he had lost.

"I am afraid that I cannot help you with the matter of your memory, sadly..." Lord Thornbridge took a deep breath. "Mayhap simply by being here, by being back in London and part of society, you might find yourself recalling some situation or another."

His bones seemed to ache with discouragement as Thomas closed his eyes.

"No. There is nothing I remember. I asked my solicitors for a detailed report of my actions, and they have given it to me, but still, there is not one single second that comes back to my mind - even though, apparently, I was quite coherent. *And,* I might add, entirely alone."

"I did not know that." Lord Thornbridge threw back his brandy and then set the glass down. "There was no one there with you then? No one encouraging you to do as they asked? No one demanding that you sign your documents?"

Thomas shook his head. The laughter and the smiles and the jovial conversation which flowed all around him seemed to bite down upon the heaviness in his heart, making it all the more weighted. He could no longer be a part of that, he realized. He could no longer be the carefree gentleman enjoying the company and the smiles of every young lady – or of one in particular – before dancing and laughing and making the most of every single joyous moment. There could be no happiness for him, not any longer.

"There must have been a reason for you to walk into your solicitors' office and to demand the entirety of your fortune."

A dark chuckle broke from Thomas' lips.

"They could not give me an explanation, I am afraid."

"And what coin do you have left, if you do not mind me asking?"

Thomas' gut twisted.

"I have a little, but it is certainly nowhere near enough to keep me in comfort for the rest of my days. It is not even enough to make certain that the estate will be profitable for the next five years." Something burned in his throat. "I am quite in the depths."

"We will find a way to pull you out."

Lord Thornbridge's voice held a good deal of determination that Thomas himself did not yet feel. There was a confidence there that he could not allow to penetrate his heart, for fear that it would give him hope. Such hope would bring him courage and that courage, in the end, would be ultimately destroyed. It would tear him down, break him apart, and send him into such a dark place that he feared he would never be free from it, would never be able to be rescued. No, he considered, it was best for him to continue on as he had been doing these last few weeks: to face the truth of his circumstances, and to look at his future with every expectation of it being just as difficult as he believed it would be.

His gaze snagged on Lady Charlotte again, her hair burning gold under the flickering candlelight. Thomas' heart lurched towards her. She was quite the beauty, and the conversations which they had shared thus far had been more than pleasant. Alas, she now represented everything that he would have to give up, every notion of happiness which would be stolen from him. His jaw tight, he forced his gaze away, only to see Lord Thornbridge's questioning look.

"It is nothing."

Lord Thornbridge shrugged.

"I did not say a single word."

Thomas managed the first genuine smile he had placed upon his lips that evening.

"You did not need to. Yes, I may have had an interest in Lady Charlotte, but that is all that it was. I am glad that there was nothing of significance between us, for it will be easy now to turn away from her – and from every young lady in London, in fact."

A small, knowing smile played about Lord Thornbridge's lips, but he said nothing. Thomas nodded to himself, as though determining that this was precisely what he was to do, steeling himself against the desire to look back in Lady Charlotte's direction.

"I will never be able to think of anything if I allow my

mind to go to places where it can never find true happiness," he told Lord Thornbridge. "From this moment I am an impoverished fellow with no fortune, and no future." Holding up both hands, he shrugged, his heart dropping to the floor, crushed under the heels of society. "What is it that I could possibly offer any young lady here? I am worth nothing. I have nothing, and nothing is all that I shall ever be."

CHAPTER FOUR

There is something about Lord Silverton which is unsettling me.

Charlotte looked steadily back at her reflection as her maid finished the final few touches to her hair for the evening. She had overheard a little of what he was speaking about with Lord Thornbridge the previous evening and had been slightly upset to hear it. For him to declare himself nothing was most unsettling. Why should he say such a thing? Lord Silverton had, to her mind, appeared despondent for the entirety of the evening. He had barely smiled, had made little attempt to converse with anyone, and had never stepped out to dance, not even once. There were certainly many young ladies who expected him to do so, but he had not obliged them. Instead, he had stayed in the corner of the ballroom, mostly with Lord Thornbridge, and had merely glanced around the room. He showed no interest in any young lady, as he had previously done and, in that regard, Charlotte was a little relieved – not because she was glad of his disinterest but, selfishly, she admitted, because she was not the only one who was being subjected to his lack of interest.

I must forget him. That way I will be able to continue with my Season without any difficulty.

Settling her hands in her lap, Charlotte took a deep breath and tried to smile at her reflection, but her smile felt forced and empty. Yes, she knew full well that she ought to forget Lord Silverton, but the truth was that, now that she had overheard him speak so, her interest was piqued all the more. It was foolish indeed to allow herself to feel such curiosity, especially when he had told her that he had no interest in her at all, but she could not seem to help it. He went around and around in her mind and, no matter what she did or thought, there he remained, just waiting for her to consider him again.

"You look quite beautiful this evening, my Lady."

The maid stepped back, her hands tight together, and Charlotte looked steadily at her reflection. Clear blue eyes looked back at her with her golden hair atop her head like a crown. Gentle curls touched her ears and temples, but her lips were a little pursed. Forcing one, she caught the look of relief on the maid's expression, fleeting as it was, and set her shoulders a little lower. She did not want the servant to think that *she* was the cause of Charlotte's frustration this evening.

"You have done a very fine job." Rising from her chair, she smiled again. "I thank you."

The door opened just as Charlotte finished speaking and her mother swung in, her hands immediately outstretched.

"Goodness, Charlotte, you are not even dressed!"

"It will not take but a moment, Mama." Charlotte gestured to her maid, who quickly scurried off to fetch the gown so that Charlotte might step into it. "There is nothing wrong I hope?"

"We must speak before we go." Lady Landon sent a quick glance in the direction of the maid, making it clear that she was not willing to speak to Charlotte until they were quite alone. Understanding this, Charlotte focused solely on donning her gown, ready for the evening. Her heart quickened a little as she caught the severe look on her mother's face and there came not even a hint of a smile when Charlotte stood ready. No flicker of happiness brightened Lady Landon's eyes.

Whatever was wrong?

"You may go." Dismissing the maid, Lady Landon waited until the door was shut tight before she stood a little closer to Charlotte. There was a firm glint in her gaze and Charlotte held her breath, suddenly afraid that she had made some mistake that her mother was now about to rail at her for. Such a thing had only happened once during the previous Season, when she had spoken a little too openly during one particular conversation when three gentlemen were present, alongside her mother and Lady Florence... and Charlotte had not forgotten what had come thereafter. Back then, her mother had held the very same glint in her eye as was there now. What was it that she had done? "I saw you speaking with Lord Silverton last evening."

A quick breath escaped Charlotte before she pulled more air into her tight lungs.

"Yes, Mama."

Was this what it was to be? A reminder that she was not to become too close with Lord Silverton, that there were other gentlemen in London who might capture her attention?

Taking a couple of steps closer, Lady Landon took Charlotte's hand, pressing it firmly.

"You are to stay away from him."

Charlotte frowned.

"What do you mean?"

More than a little confused. Charlotte held her mother's gaze, who quickly gave a slight shake of her head.

"What I have just said to you is what I mean. I do not think I can make myself clearer than that."

Charlotte's frown lingered, her intrigue growing.

"I understand, Mama, that you do not want me to go near Lord Silverton again, but you have not given me a reason for such a thing."

Lady Landon tilted her chin up a little.

"The last I knew, Charlotte, I was your mother and therefore not obliged to give you explanations, no matter how much you might desire them."

Charlotte's eyes opened wider. She was a little taken aback, for it was most unlike her mother to speak with such sharpness.

"I did not mean –"

Closing her eyes, her mother squeezed her hand again.

"Forgive me, my dear. I should not have spoken so. It is only that I am a little surprised over what I have heard and, I confess, a little angry."

At this, a cold hand grasped at Charlotte's heart.

"Angry?"

"I am doing this in order to protect you."

"Protect me? From Lord Silverton?" Seeing her mother nod, Charlotte twisted her mouth to one side, rather confused as to why her mother would need to protect her from the gentleman. "Has something happened, Mama?"

Lady Landon hesitated.

"I –"

"Has something been revealed about Lord Silverton, something which was as yet unknown to society about his character? Has he done something so severe that you must now encourage me away from him?"

Understanding cleared Lady Landon's expression at once.

"There is nothing of Lord Silverton's character that need concern you, my dear. He has not turned out to be a rogue or a scoundrel, or any such thing as that, so you may put that from your mind." A good deal relieved, Charlotte closed her eyes for a moment and let out a full breath, calming her nerves. "There is no need to go into particular detail, " Lady Landon continued. "What I will say, however, is that I am demanding such a thing from you so that I might make certain of your happiness." Her hard expression gentled. "You are my only daughter. I want what is the very best for you."

"And you do not consider Lord Silverton to be a suitable gentleman for me?"

Her mother shook her head.

"I am afraid that I do not, and neither does your father." The firm tone with which her mother spoke gave Charlotte a clear understanding of what her acquaintance with Lord Silverton could be. There could be a brief murmur of greeting, one or two quiet interactions, but nothing of any length or intimacy. The conversations she had enjoyed with him thus far could no longer continue. For whatever reason, both her parents had decided that he was not a suitable acquaintance for her any longer, although Charlotte could not imagine why such a thing could be. What was it that Lord Silverton had done to merit such behavior? "Do you understand, Charlotte?"

Aware that she would not be given any further clarification, Charlotte nodded. There was nothing else for her to do but agree.

"Yes, Mama."

Lady Landon smiled.

"Thank you, my dear. Be aware that you are not the only one to be doing such a thing – there will be other young ladies also, but it is for good reason. Keep your interactions with him brief. Cordial but not friendly. Do you understand?"

"Yes. I will do as you have requested, Mama."

Stepping forward, her mother embraced her gently.

"I thank you. Come now, let us make our way to the ball and hope that what I have asked of you will not cause any difficulty... either for you or for Lord Silverton." Her eyes narrowed. "Hopefully, he will understand."

Still greatly confused, Charlotte followed her mother, making her way toward the staircase which would take her to the waiting carriage. Her mind, however, was not settled, not in any way. Yes, she had told her mother that she would do as had been asked, but that did not mean that she was fully committed to doing so. If an opportunity came, then she might very well ask Lord Silverton about this matter.

Why must I stay far from him?

If it was not to do with Lord Silverton's character, if he was not a secret rake nor a rascal, then why would her mother possibly push her so firmly away from him? Try as she might, Charlotte could not force him from her thoughts, despite her promise to her mother, not even as they sat in the carriage on the way to the ball. One thing for certain, however; she would make sure to greet him this evening, albeit very quietly and very briefly! Mayhap, she reasoned, in doing so, she would find a clue as to why she was now to separate herself from the one gentleman she had ever been interested in.

～

"Good evening." Charlotte grabbed Lady Florence's arm, taking her away from both of their mothers who stood talking together. "Might we take a turn about the room?"

Lady Florence's smile disappeared.

"Of course." Her gaze fixed itself on Charlotte. "Is there something wrong?"

Leaning a little closer. Charlotte looked back steadily at her friend.

"Do you know the reason I must stay away from Lord Silverton?"

Lady Florence's eyes flared.

"Your mother has asked you to stay away from him?"

Nodding, Charlotte began to wander around the room with Lady Florence beside her, going carefully and slowly so that they might speak together.

"Yes, she has." Seeing that Lady Florence was as puzzled as she, Charlotte let out a long breath. "It is most confusing. She would not give me a reason, but at the same time, stated that it was nothing to do with Lord Silverton's character. I have not misjudged him in any way, which was something of a relief, at least."

Lady Florence shook her head.

"I had not heard of any reason why Lord Silverton should be pushed away from society."

"I do not think that he is being given the cut direct or anything like that," Charlotte replied quickly. "To my mind, it appears as though he is just as welcome within society as before, but there will be those who are no longer as eager for his company as they once were. Again, I am uncertain as to the reason for such behavior. My mother would give me no cause for it."

"Are *you* to give him the cut direct then, even if others will not?"

Laughing, Charlotte shook her head.

"No, my dear friend, it is not as severe as that. My mother has said that I may be genial but there is to be no prolonged conversation. I am not to remain or linger in his company, not for any reason."

A light came into Lady Florence's eyes.

"Which of course, makes him all the more mysterious."

Attempting to form a serious expression, Charlotte held her head high.

"I am going to do as my mother has stated," she said firmly. "I have every intention of doing as she asks... although I also intend to take careful note of Lord Silverton."

Lady Florence giggled.

"I knew that you could not be as obedient as that!"

Charlotte rolled her eyes.

"I confess that my curiosity has been nudged. I do not think that I can simply accept this new separation without knowing the reason for it."

"No, of course you cannot!" Lady Florence exclaimed. "I shall aid you, of course, in any way that I can."

"You do not think me foolish, then? After all, Lord Silverton and I were only acquainted. There was never a connection between us, never even a mention of such a thing."

"But as we have already determined, you are a little interested in the gentleman," Lady Florence reminded her with a small smile. "So yes, there is good reason to do such a thing and no, I do not think you foolish." Her eyes darted across the room as if to look for the gentleman in question, with her fingers tightening on Charlotte's arm. "In fact..."

Following her friend's gaze, Charlotte looked over her shoulder just to see Lord Silverton looking back toward her. Her heart slammed against her chest, and a moment was shared between them, a moment where Lord Silverton acknowledged her with a small yet cool smile, and she lowered her eyes before lifting them, gazing back at him in return.

And then she immediately turned her head away so that she would not have to look at Lord Silverton any longer. Heat was burning in her face, and Lady Florence was laughing softly, obviously aware of the effect that Lord Silverton had upon Charlotte.

"Let us turn around and go to greet him!" Lady Florence urged. "We need not make it look obvious, but it would be good to make sure that we have spoken to him this evening."

"Alas, I cannot be seen to be doing so," Charlotte, reminded her friend, but Lady Florence only began to walk a little more quickly, turning them both around.

"I said I would help you, did I not?" Gaining a little speed, Lady Florence's determination was demonstrated by her swift actions. "I will make certain that you are not seen by your mother, nor by mine. My mother has said no such thing to me, I might add."

"That is because you already have a particular gentle-man," Charlotte reminded her. "My mother is quite determined to make certain that Lord Silverton is not the person I consider. Perhaps, if your mother says something to you about the matter, you would be able to inform me of what is said?"

"But of course."

Slowing their steps, the two meandered towards Lord Silverton. He was speaking with a smaller group of both gentlemen and ladies, but rather than leave, Lady Florence moved them both into the circle and, within a few minutes, they had an opportunity to greet each and every person in that particular group.

Charlotte made her way around each person, leaving Lord Silverton until the last. Her eyes held to his as he looked back at her, his expression blank. She could not even guess as to what he was thinking.

"And good evening to you also, Lord Silverton."

She stepped a little to her left, thinking to secure herself in front of an overly tall and rather broad fellow who would hide her from her mother's gaze. Lady Landon, however, appeared still to be in deep discussion with Lady Florence's mother, and Charlotte prayed that she would remain so for the next few minutes at least.

"Good evening, Lady Charlotte." Immediately, Lord Silverton took his gaze away, saying nothing more. The conversation continued to flow around her, but Charlotte could not help but keep her gaze steadily on his face, questions folding, one after the other, into her mind, going into every empty space. What was it that he had done? Why had her mother been so eager to pull her away from him and, at their last meeting, why had he been so very dismissive? It was all very strange indeed. "Is there a reason that you are staring at me, Lady Charlotte?"

Blinking rapidly, Charlotte realized that Lord Silverton had moved toward her as she had been staring at him. Her thoughts had been so many that she had not even realized he had moved closer. Taking a breath, she chose to be brave.

"Yes, Lord Silverton, there is."

A small smile crept up the edges of Lord Silverton's mouth.

"And might you tell me what that reason is?"

Charlotte considered this, looking up into his handsome face. His brown eyes were a little darker than she remembered them, or mayhap it was his dark hair that spread so low to his eyes that gave such an impression.

"The last time we spoke, Lord Silverton, you were most dismissive."

She did not ask any questions, but simply looked back at him without blinking, catching how the corners of his mouth drooped. The silence grew between them for some moments, but Charlotte made no attempt to break it. Would this be the moment when he would say something, would reveal to her the reason that her mother had told her to distance herself from him?

Eventually, Lord Silverton blew out a heavy breath and turned his head away.

"I was a little rude, yes."

His eyes caught hers again, and he gave no further reason for his behavior, just as her mother had given her no reason for her request. Becoming a little exasperated, Charlotte clenched one hand but kept her expression calm.

"That is no apology."

The smile became a little rueful.

"No, I suppose it was not. Perhaps in attempting to be honest, I came across a little impolite. I apologize for that."

In being honest?

Charlotte's stomach twisted around as she looked back at him, seeing how his shoulders dropped and his smile faded. Evidently, he *had* been disinterested in her then. It had not just been a remark which had been said and regretted, as she had hoped.

"I should not be speaking with you."

Murmuring to herself, Charlotte turned her head away and made to move across towards Lady Florence, who had somehow, in the course of Charlotte's conversation with Lord Silverton, moved away from her. Much to her astonishment, however, a hand grasped hers and pulled her back.

Turning rapidly, she tugged her hand away, terrified now that her mother would see what had happened. A quick glance over towards Lady Landon brought great relief to that concern for Charlotte, for her mother was still close to Lady Davenport, talking in depth about something – mayhap talking of Lord Silverton himself.

"What do you mean, you ought not to be speaking with me?"

Turning her attention back to Lord Silverton, Charlotte's breath caught in her chest at the swirling darkness in his eyes.

"It is precisely as I have said. I have been asked to make certain that my acquaintance with you is not of any consequence. A brief greeting, a few pleasant words certainly, but that is all that I am to do."

Lord Silverton's jaw jutted forward.

"I must know what you mean. I must know *why*."

Looking around the room as if he were afraid that whatever they spoke of would be overheard by a good many people, he reached again to grasp at her hand. Instead, his fingers closed around her wrist and, much to her astonishment, Charlotte was tugged gently after him. She should not go, yet to resist could make a scene, and she could not allow that for fear of drawing attention. After just a moment, she therefore found her feet going willingly. No matter the turmoil in her thoughts. Throwing a glance behind her, she caught Lady Florence's eye, and her friend gave a sharp nod before following her at some distance.

Having very little idea of where Lord Silverton was intending to take her, Charlotte swallowed against the knot in her throat. It would be wise to step back but, at the present moment, she was much too curious to pull herself away.

The moment they reached the side of the ballroom, where they were hidden in amongst the shadows of a cluster of potted palms, Lord Silverton turned around to face her, his hand releasing her wrist.

"You have been told to stay away from me. Is that what you were saying?"

Trying to catch her breath, Charlotte managed a small nod, relieved to see that Lady Florence stood only a few steps away. Her friend did not come near, however, allowing the conversation between Lord Silverton and Charlotte to continue uninterrupted.

"I knew that this would happen." Pushing both hands through his brown hair, Lord Silverton blew out a harsh breath between clenched teeth. "And what has been said about me?"

Charlotte blinked.

"Nothing."

Lord Silverton looked back steadily, unbelief staring at her through his eyes.

"You need not try to protect my feelings, Lady Charlotte. I know that something will have been said. Pray tell me what it is. Tell me what it is at once."

Finding herself moving closer out of concern for his obvious distress, Charlotte put one hand on his arm, and immediately Lord Silverton seemed to fold in on himself a little. His shoulders dropped, the air left his lips in a long rush, and his eyes softened.

"I speak the truth, Lord Silverton. My mother has said very little to me about why I am to stay distant from you. She *has* stated, however, that it is nothing to do with your character, that you are not a scoundrel or any such thing."

Lord Silverton closed his eyes as though she had said something greatly injuring.

"I suppose that is something of a relief."

Muttering words that she could not make out, he turned his head away, and Charlotte let her hand remain on his arm. He needed comfort and she could not step away from him now, no matter what her mother had told her to do.

"I do not understand, Lord Silverton." Keeping her voice soft, she spoke eagerly, wondering if now she might discover the answer to the mystery. "Is the fact that you have been so disagreeable towards me and, thereafter, my mother now encouraging me to stay far from you related in any way?"

Turning his attention back towards her, Lord Silverton pulled his arm gently behind his back so that she was forced to release him. They were close, however – perhaps a little too close, given the way that her breath caught in her chest. Clearing his throat, Lord Silverton lifted his chin a little so that their faces were not so near to each other, but Charlotte's heart beat all the more quickly regardless.

"It is best that you do what your mother has asked you." Giving her no further explanation, this was followed by a quick bow. "I am sorry that I pulled you over here in such a disgraceful manner. That was not right of me, and I apologize profusely."

Her heart dropped.

This is all I am to know?

It looked as though he was about to make his way past her, but without hesitating, Charlotte sidestepped him so that he could not escape.

"Pray, do not leave me alone to stand here and look after you and wonder what it is that is going on. Why is it that my mother has asked me to distance myself from you? If it is not of your character, then what else could it possibly be?"

Catching her fingers briefly, Lord Silverton pressed them for a moment, silencing her questions.

"This is not something which need concern you. Do what your mother has asked. I shall do the same and make certain not to come close to you again."

Pain stabbed at her heart.

"And what if I should not want that?"

Lord Silverton gave her a small smile – a smile that did not touch his eyes.

"I am afraid that you must accept it regardless. I will be withdrawing from *every* eligible lady, not just yourself. Believe me, that is for the best." His smile cracked and he looked away, heaving a heavy sigh which seemed to come from the very depths of his soul. "Good evening, Lady Charlotte."

Having nothing else to say, Charlotte turned and watched him depart, all the more confused as to what it was that was taking place with Lord Silverton. He had seemed relieved to know that it was not his character that was being called into question, but he obviously was still aware of why her mother had ordered that she stay away from him. The fact that she had no answer as yet was deeply frustrating and, despite the fact that both her mother, and now Lord Silverton himself, had asked for her to distance herself, Charlotte did not allow her curiosity to fade. His upset distressed her, and she silently swore that she would not leave the matter alone.

Lady Florence came towards her.

"I did not hear a word of what was said. Did you find satisfaction, however?"

"I am afraid I did not." Sighing quietly, Charlotte turned back to her friend. "Before you ask, my interest is not sated. In fact, I would say it is all the stronger, but I cannot be seen talking to him when both he and my mother are now quite insistent that I do not!"

Lady Florence gasped, clearly a little taken aback.

"Lord Silverton himself has asked you to remain far from his company?"

Glancing over her shoulder towards the retreating figure of Lord Silverton, Charlotte's heart turned over on itself, seeing that he had already been swallowed up by the crowd.

"He told me that he would be keeping himself apart from every lady in London – every unattached lady that is. I am included in that."

"That is very strange." Reaching out to squeeze Charlotte's hand, Lady Florence gave her a quick smile. "I am not surprised that your curiosity is further piqued. I find that my own interest is also caught by this matter!"

"You will not berate me then?"

Giving her friend a slightly rueful smile, Charlotte looked back at Lady Florence rather than attempt to make out Lord Silverton in the crowd.

"Certainly, I shall not. In fact, I believe that I would be quite disappointed if you had no interest in the matter, although I would beg of you to be careful. You do have a reputation to take care of and your mother will be very cross indeed should she discover that you are not doing as she has asked."

"I would agree." Taking a deep breath. Charlotte forced her attention to turn to the ball rather than thinking continually about Lord Silverton. "In speaking of my mother's ire, I find myself aware that I ought to consider the rest of the evening. My dance card has no names on it as yet, and my mother will be most displeased if it continues to be so!"

"And I am sure that you, yourself, would enjoy the evening a little more if you have some gentlemen to dance and converse with." Her friend smiled softly. "For all that Lord Silverton has caught your interest, you may discover that there is someone else who captures you in an entirely different way – and then you need not think of him any longer. You can leave him to whatever he is doing at present without concern."

Considering, Charlotte let her gaze fly over the crowd, accepting all that her friend had to say. All the same, however, this desire to find out why Lord Silverton was removing his company from her and from every other eligible young lady remained. With a small sigh, she turned and looped her hand through her friend's arm.

"Come then. Let us go and see if I can find at least *one* gentleman to sign my dance card!"

"I am certain you shall have it filled within the hour!" Lady Florence replied with a smile. "And who knows, you may find something out, hear some whisper or other that will give an answer to your wish to know the secret of Lord Silverton."

Laughing, Charlotte shook her head.

"Mayhap you are right," she answered. "I can only hope that such a wish will come true."

CHAPTER FIVE

"*A*nd how went your investigation?"

Thomas rolled his eyes.

"Very badly."

Lord Pottinger sent him a rueful smile.

"I am sorry to hear that. What have you done thus far?"

Thomas spread his hands, shrugging.

"I have visited the gambling den. I have spoken to the proprietor. Nothing came to mind. No instant memory returned to me, no quick thought. No recollection of anything, in fact."

"That is disappointing."

"But not unexpected. As I have said, I could not recall anything from that evening. Therefore, it would come as a great surprise to me to remember anything more, simply because I visited the place that we went to that evening."

"All the same, that must be difficult for you." Rising, Lord Pottinger made his way across the room to look out of the window. "I had expected Lord and Lady Foster to have already arrived, but as yet they have not. They are a little tardy and that is not at all like them."

Thomas sighed.

"Allow them to be late, Pottinger. They are newlyweds, after all."

Lord Pottinger nodded, made his way back across the room, and slumped back down in his chair.

"You are quite right. I suppose it is a little unsettling, this present situation, and I am allowing it to play on my mind."

A slight frown dusted across Thomas' forehead.

"What is it about this circumstance in particular that you are finding difficult? Surely you are quite contented with things as they are now, given that you have gained your fortune again."

"It is not my situation which concerns me, but rather yours," Lord Pottinger explained. "We are all eager to help you. It would not sit well with us if we all recovered our fortunes, only to see you struggling. I believe that there is an agreement that we would not allow you to linger in poverty, even if we were unable to find the culprit."

At this, Thomas fervently shook his head.

"Please do not. I could not imagine having to pay back debts to any of my friends."

"It would not be debt we offer you, but gifts, with no expectation of repayment ever being required. None of us would be pleased to see you in such a situation, not when we were also tricked." Something tightened in Thomas' chest, and he drew his eyes away from his friends, caught somewhere between embarrassment and gladness. The kindness his friends were showing him was marvelous in itself, but to be told that he would not always be in this dire situation, regardless of the outcome here in London, was a great relief indeed. At the same time, however, his pride demanded that he refuse. "Do not even think that you cannot accept." A broad smile settled across Lord Pottinger's face. "I can tell by the tightness of your jaw and the way your eyes glance from one side of the room to the other that you do not want to accept, but at the very same time, I know that you would be very glad of it. Regardless, I do not think that you will have a choice. One way or the other, you will be quite secure, even if it means that we, as your friends, have a little less."

Seeing the steel glint in Lord Pottinger's eye, Thomas could tell that there was no point in arguing. His friends would find a way to put their money into his pocket.

"I am grateful." Still keeping his head turned away, Thomas let out a slow breath. "I should not want everyone to think that I am ungrateful."

"No one would think this of you, I assure you."

At that same moment, the drawing room door was flung open, and Lord Foster practically fell into the room, swiftly followed by Lady Foster. Thomas rose at once, on instinct, with Lord Pottinger hurrying to lead Lady Foster to a chair – although she did not seem in need of him, waving one hand furiously in Lord Foster's direction, just as Lord Foster exclaimed something that Thomas could not quite understand.

"I am certain! I am certain it was him."

"It was a passing carriage," Lady Foster said, as she sat down. "You might have been mistaken."

"I know who it was I saw - I would not forget that man's face."

It was obvious to Thomas' eyes that Lady Foster bit back her reply, for her lips pressed hard together and her hands folded tightly in her lap.

"A brandy, perhaps?"

Lord Pottinger glanced first at Lord Foster and then

toward Thomas, who nodded, still keeping his gaze firmly on Lord Foster as he paced up and down the room. Something had clearly agitated the fellow, but as yet he was not making any sense.

"What is it you have seen?" Speaking quietly, Thomas lowered himself into a chair. "I can see that something has upset you."

"Not something but someone." Lord Foster threw out a hand toward his wife. "My dear lady did not see it, for she was a little behind me. But I am certain that it was *him* I saw."

Lord Pottinger handed Thomas a brandy, and then took a glass towards Lord Foster before looking enquiringly at Lady Foster. She shook her head, and Lord Pottinger rang the bell instead, intending to send for tea for the lady.

"I thought that he was on the continent!" Muttering to himself, Lord Foster took a small sip of his brandy. "He must have returned."

Air seemed to lodge itself in Thomas' throat for a moment, stopping his breath, as he stared at Lord Foster, finally able to understand what the man meant. Lord Pottinger also stood stock still, staring first at Lord Foster, and then looking inquiringly towards Lady Foster. She gave a gentle shrug of her shoulders, but remained silent, leaving Thomas to ask the question that he was sure was on both his and Lord Pottinger's minds.

"You are trying to suggest that you saw Lord Montague."

Lord Foster turned to Thomas, his brandy slopping to one side of his glass such was the speed with which he turned.

"I am not *suggesting* anything. I am telling you that I saw the man sitting in a carriage. I was merely walking down the street towards your house, Lord Pottinger, when my attention was caught by a loud and abrasive laugh. In the noise of the crowd, I was rather surprised to hear such a thing, but it was only when I turned that I caught sight of Lord Montague's face. It was not he who was laughing, however, but because my attention had been drawn in that direction, his was the face that I saw."

Thomas' fingers gripped the glass. Lord Montague had been the one who had not only stolen from Lord Foster but who also killed Lord Gillespie. Yes, Lord Gillespie had been the one to lead them to the East End of London, taking them to that gambling den, and by now they were all well aware that he'd had a hand in everything which had taken place, but that did not mean that he had deserved death, of course.

Lord Montague was a cruel man.

"I do not understand what he would be doing back in London." Lady Foster spoke quietly, in a tone that was either meant to calm or placate her husband... or perhaps maybe both. "We knew that he was going to the continent. He had gone to escape any further consequences that might have come about should he remain in England. You made yourself very clear when you last met with him."

"I am well aware that I did." Lord Foster finally dropped into a chair, leaning forward so that his head might drop between his knees for a moment as he let out a low groan. "My manservant, David, and his family are currently removing to my estate, whilst I myself remain here in London. Had he been here, then I might have sent him out to Lord Montague's townhouse and various other places to make *certain* as to whether or not Montague is present."

"Surely it would take something of great significance to draw him back to England, and specifically to London?"

Thomas remarked quietly. "And my guess would be that he would not be in his townhouse or any of his usual haunts, not if he is attempting to keep himself hidden from the *ton's* eyes whilst here in London. He could not make himself known to society, not after so many of them now know the truth about his character."

Lord Pottinger took a small sip of his brandy and then stared down into the depths of his glass, evidently considering. Silence fell across the room, leaving each gentleman and lady to their own thoughts. After some minutes, Lord Pottinger was the first to break it.

"Was he with anyone in the carriage?"

"Not that I was able to see." Lord Foster shook his head, running one hand through his dark hair as he finally lifted his gaze. "It was only a glimpse. My dear wife is not at all sure that it was him... and now that I have had some time, perhaps I am wrong in what I saw."

Given the strength of Lord Foster's reaction, Thomas was not certain that the man had been mistaken. The fact that he had initially been so clearly determined that it had been none other than Lord Montague was enough to convince Thomas.

"I am asking you only to be cautious." Lady Foster now sounded a little upset, clearly distressed about all that was taking place. "I am not stating that you were wrong, only asking you to take some moments to truly consider what you saw." Leaning forward, she clasped her hands in her lap as she gazed earnestly at her husband. "Is there even the smallest doubt in your mind, Foster? Regardless of what I have said, what is fixed in your mind?"

A burst of energy ran around the room as a long quiet followed. Thomas sucked in air, breathing slowly and carefully whilst trying to maintain his composure, his hands flexing. If Lord Foster truly *had* seen Lord Montague, then the situation had taken a very different turn. There would be a good many questions and, no doubt, a determination to know why the man was back in town.

Taking a deep breath, Lord Foster let it out carefully so that the sound filled the room. It was as though he wanted to make certain that everyone believed he was being considered before he gave his response, but the answer was just as Thomas had expected.

"There is not a single flicker of uncertainty in my mind." Drawing in another deep breath, he sat up straight, slapping his hands on his thighs. "That *was* Lord Montague. Lord Montague is back in London."

A certain thought grasped Thomas' mind and he cleared his throat, drawing the attention of everyone. A little embarrassed, he quickly spread his hands.

"It is just a mere thought, but did we not make certain that Lord Montague had gone to the continent?"

"Yes." Lord Foster confirmed. "David, my manservant, made sure that he was taken to the ship. Indeed, I recall him stating that he had not left the dock until the ship with Lord Montague aboard set sail."

Nodding slowly, Thomas thought quickly.

"So we are certain that Lord Montague left England. That is without question. However, my consideration now is that he may have found a way from the ship to come back to England. For all we know, he may have been lying low somewhere in England ever since and did not return to town until this moment. I cannot imagine why he has done so, but he could not have gone to the continent and returned again within such a short time. He must have made his escape. He must have come back to English shores far sooner than we ever realized."

Lord Foster let out a low groan.

"And like a fool, I believed that he had gone where I had sent him. I did not even consider that he might try to do something else."

"You are no fool." Lady Foster answered quickly, replicating Thomas' thought. "You did everything which was required of you." Letting out a sigh, she ran one hand over her eyes. "Now that Lord Silverton has explained to me what Lord Montague could have done, I can see that the situation might be a little more dire than we had expected. There is every possibility, I suppose, that Lord Montague has returned."

"It is dangerous for him to be here." Thomas remarked as the other gentleman nodded. "There is the threat that Lord Foster hung over his head. I do not think that he will have forgotten it."

"Which perhaps will mean that he will do everything he can to make certain that his presence here in London is not noticed by many." Lord Pottinger shrugged both shoulders. "He is wily enough, we know that for certain. I believe that he will do everything he can to hide his true intentions from everybody until, mayhap, it is too late."

Lord Foster nodded slowly as Thomas let his gaze turn from one to the other. If Lord Montague was now back in London, then that was of great concern to them all, but to Lord Foster more than any. He had believed, as they all had, that Lord Montague had been on his way to the continent and would not return to England for some time – years, in fact. Now it seemed as though the man had tricked them once again.

"We must fix all of our attention upon this matter," he said quietly as Lord Foster immediately began to shake his head. "I will not brook any argument, Foster. I know exactly what this man means to you *and* what he has done, and I will not allow my thoughts to turn towards anything else – not even to my own fortune."

"There is no need for that," Lord Foster began to protest, but Thomas merely held up one hand.

"I have already heard from Lord Pottinger about your intentions for my ongoing security, should my fortune not be recovered," he replied quietly. "Allow me to show the same kindness in return. Perhaps, in time, I will be able to recover my fortune, but for the moment, this issue is a good deal more pressing. Who knows?" Lifting both shoulders, he gave his friend a small smile. "This may give me some insight."

Lord Foster managed to return Thomas' smile, albeit a little ruefully.

"It is the least we can hope for, I suppose." Sitting up a little straighter, he looked first at Lady Foster, then at Thomas again. "I thank you, my friend. Your generosity does not go unnoticed."

Thomas said nothing, taking the first sip of his brandy and letting it warm him as he considered the difficulties they faced. For the moment, he would have to set his own investigations to the side, thinking only of Lord Montague and his return to society.

It would not mean, however, that he would be able to simply return to society as he had done before. His conversation with Lady Charlotte had not left his mind, for he was quite sure now that everyone in London was aware of his circumstances and that, in due course, they would turn their backs on him – save only for his friends.

"Speaking of this situation, have you made any progress?"

Thomas shook his head in response to Lord Foster's question.

"But I am certain that the *ton* knows that I am impoverished." Letting out a frustrated breath. He allowed the heavy sigh to fill the room for a few moments. "I had a recent conversation with Lady Charlotte where she informed me that her mother stated that she was no longer to be in my company."

"And you believe that it is because of this situation with your fortune?"

A dark bark of laughter ripped from Thomas' throat in answer to Lord Pottinger's question.

"What other reason could there be? It may be rumor at present, but I believe that will only last for so long."

Lady Foster reached across and pressed his hand for just a moment, with her soft smile a gentle balm to his present frustration and upset.

"You will find that we all understand such a difficulty," she answered him softly. "And we understand all that you feel."

For whatever reason, a vision of Lady Charlotte came into his mind as though *she* were the one pressing his hand rather than Lady Foster. A little confused, Thomas blinked rapidly until finally his gaze cleared and Lady Foster returned to his view. Clearing his throat, he managed to smile, but said nothing in response. What had just taken place?

"You said that her mother requested that Lady Charlotte stay far from you," Lord Pottinger continued, his eyes flickering with awareness. "It is interesting, then, that she made her way to your side regardless."

Thomas shook his head.

"I would not allow her to linger near me, not for my own sake. Instead, I insisted that she do as her mother ask. I did not give her any further reasons for this, even though I am well aware that she was very confused." Seeing the light frown on Lord Foster's face, he quickly explained. "Lady Landon did not give an explanation of why her daughter had to stay away from me. Lady Charlotte came to speak to me about the matter, perhaps in the hope that I would tell her everything." A slight flush rose quickly up his chest. "I confess that I did not."

"But it is not something you need to be ashamed of, for we all understand." Lord Pottinger rose from his chair, going to fetch the brandy for Lord Foster again. "Should I hear anything, I will inform you of it at once."

"As shall I," Lord and Lady Foster said in unison, sharing a quick smile before Lord Foster's attention returned solely to Thomas. "And no matter what may happen, you know that your friends will stick by you. You shall not be shamed in this, for you will have all of us around you, defending you. You are not alone."

Thomas looked around the room and felt his heart lift a little, Despite the heaviness which came in recalling his conversation with Lady Charlotte, in spite of his difficult circumstances, he could not help but be grateful. Yes, he *did* have excellent friends who were willing to stand beside him and take some of the burden from his shoulders.

"Yes, you are right." Taking a deep breath, he allowed it to fill his lungs and bring a little relief to his tight muscles. "I am not on my own in this situation. That will be a great comfort to me in the days to come. I thank you all."

"$\mathscr{H}$e is here this evening. He has only just arrived."

Charlotte nodded, well aware of the fact that Lord Silverton was already present. She had noticed him the very moment that she had walked into the soiree, although she would not admit to the fact, not even to Lady Florence.

"Are you going to speak with him?"

Shrugging, Charlotte pretended that his presence here did not concern her a great deal. She did not want her friend to know just how intrigued she had become these last few days, nor did she want to admit to the fact that she was watching Lord Silverton carefully to make certain that what he had said about staying far from every eligible lady in London was quite true.

A sudden laugh fell from Lady Florence's lips.

"I see that you are pretending that you have no interest in Lord Silverton at present," she remarked, her eyes sparking with mirth. "Come now, we have already discussed this! You know that I will support you in your endeavors to understand the truth."

"Yes, but I am determined to remain hidden in that endeavor, recall." Charlotte glanced to Lady Florence, her friend's smile fleeting - perhaps she had forgotten Charlotte's decision? "Thus far, he has stayed away from every young lady here. There have been some that he has greeted but their conversations have been very short, and anyone he has indulged with a long conversation is either already wed or old enough to be his mother."

Again, this made Lady Florence laugh, and Charlotte allowed herself a grin. It was quite ridiculous of her to be watching Lord Silverton with such sharp eyes, but she could not help herself. It was as though she knew exactly where he was in the room at every moment, even though she was not continually setting her gaze upon him.

"That is good at least, although I would not say that Lady Denfield is in any of those particular categories. "

Charlotte's eyes immediately flew across the room towards Lord Silverton. To her surprise, she saw him in deep conversation with a lady whom she had thought was already wed and therefore, it had not concerned her until this moment. Lady Denfield was only a year or so older than Charlotte, but she was *certain* that the lady was already married.

"What do you mean? Lady Denfield was married some years ago, was she not? Mama told me of it last Season when we were introduced. Apparently, it was the talk of London, for she had only just made her come out when she found herself betrothed."

"Lord Denfield died a short while after their marriage." Lady Florence replied quietly, her mouth pulling down a little. "I believe it was rather unexpected, for Lord Denfield, while older, was nowhere near his dotage."

Swallowing hard, Charlotte studied her friend, who

gave a small nod as if confirming that everything she had said was quite true.

"I did not know." Turning her gaze back towards Lady Denfield and Lord Silverton, she studied him carefully, wondering whether or not he himself knew that the young woman he was speaking to was, in fact, a widow. "It may be that he does not know of her late husband's passing, as I was unaware," she murmured softly. "Someone should speak to him about it."

"Charlotte." The warning was heavy in Lady Florence's voice. "Pray, do not do what I *think* you are considering. It would not be wise. It–"

Before Lady Florence could say anything more, Charlotte had already begun to make her way across the room. She walked with so much energy that the hurried sounds of Lady Florence's footsteps told her that her friend had needed to quicken her steps to catch up with her. Lifting her chin and praying desperately that her mother would not be watching, she made her way toward Lord Silverton. When his eyes caught hers, her brows lifted in feigned surprise as though she had not expected to see him there, coming to a stop near where he stood with Lady Denfield.

"Good evening, Lord Silverton." With bright eyes and a bright smile, she turned back to Lady Denfield. "And good evening to you also, Lady Denfield. I do not think that we have met this Season so far."

Lady Denfield smiled, and Charlotte's heart dropped. The young woman was a beauty, with striking red hair and vivid green eyes. No doubt, she had captured the interest of many a gentleman during her come out only for her betrothal to be made known in the days after.

"Yes, you are quite correct." Lady Denfield's expression warmed gently, and a nudge of guilt pushed against Charlotte's heart, reminding her that she could have no particular upset over Lady Denfield's presence here. It was not her fault that she was so very beautiful.

"We were acquainted last Season, if I recall?"

Charlotte nodded, wishing now that she had listened a little more when her mother had spoken of Lady Denfield last year. If she had, then perhaps Charlotte might have known already that Lady Denfield was widowed.

"Yes, I believe that is so. Are you enjoying this Season?"

Lady Denfield smiled again.

"Certainly, I am." Her eyes flicked towards Lord Silverton – a gesture that Charlotte did not miss. "It has been very pleasant greeting all of my acquaintances... and making new ones."

A flare of interest rose in Charlotte's chest, lighting her eyes and opening them a little more.

"You mean to say that you have only just become acquainted with Lord Silverton?" Her eyes went from one to the other, just as Lord Silverton nodded. A smile flitted across his lips, but Charlotte did not believe that it truly came from his heart. Perhaps he felt this moment awkward. Mayhap she had interrupted their very first conversation. Her stomach twisted as she dropped her gaze from his face. "I am sorry to have interrupted you both."

Genuinely meaning every word, she made to take her leave, only for Lady Denfield to laugh and catch her arm.

"Please, there is no need for you to rush away. Tell me, have you any suitors this Season? A young lady as charming and as beautiful as you surely ought to have at least three gentlemen eager to court her!"

Heat warmed Charlotte's face.

"You are very kind." She did not answer the question, however, changing the subject quickly. "And are you quite contented, Lady Denfield? After your sad circumstances, some years ago, are you still quite secure?"

Lady Denfield's green eyes flared for a moment, but the next second, she pressed one hand to her heart.

"You have such a kindness, Lady Charlotte. My late husband made certain in his will to take care of my future. I have no need at present... save perhaps, for a little more company, although that is why one comes to London, I suppose."

Charlotte sent a glance towards Lord Silverton as Lady Denfield smiled and he murmured something in return. As she watched, however, a frown slowly began to settle over his expression, and Charlotte's heart lifted. Obviously, he had been unaware that Lady Denfield was widowed, and she could not blame his lack of understanding. They had only just become acquainted and, while she regretted coming to stand in the midst of their first conversation, her heart was glad indeed that she had been able to speak so honestly about the situation. At least Lord Silverton would know now that his conversations with Lady Denfield could not continue for much longer.

Someone tapped her on the shoulder and Charlotte turned quickly, seeing Lady Florence standing there.

"Pray excuse me, but your mother requests to speak with you. Immediately."

Charlotte's stomach dropped, knowing full well why her mother required her. She would be displeased with what Charlotte had done in speaking with Lord Silverton, but Charlotte shrugged off any kind of guilt. This had been important, and her conversation had done exactly as she had hoped. Any berating from her mother was worth it.

"But of course."

Turning back to face Lady Denfield and Lord Silverton,

she smiled first at one and then at the other, but only Lady Denfield returned it.

"Pray excuse me. My mother requires me."

Lady Denfield tipped her head.

"It was very pleasant to speak with you again, Lady Charlotte."

"And with you also. Good evening."

Lord Silverton said nothing, giving her no response, save for a small nod. Turning, Charlotte made her way directly back towards her mother, with Lady Florence falling into step beside her.

"I am afraid that your mother is most displeased, for she saw you speaking with Lord Silverton and asked me to go to fetch you back to her. It seems that even *she* does not want to be in Lord Silverton's company."

Keeping her voice low, Charlotte cast a quick glance toward her friend.

"I believe that such an act of defiance was worth it, however," she answered quietly. "Lord Silverton was clearly unaware that Lady Denfield was a widow. I mentioned her sad circumstances and the surprise on his face was obvious to all."

There was no time to say anything further, for they had reached both Lady Landon and Lady Davenport, with Lady Florence stepping away immediately to stand by her mother. Lady Landon immediately began to berate Charlotte for going anywhere near Lord Silverton. Charlotte replied that she had been speaking to Lady Denfield and could not simply step away from her because of Lord Silverton's presence, and, to her relief, this seemed to calm her mother a little, although her upset remained.

"In this circumstance you may well have been acting correctly, but that does not mean that I am pleased." Lady

Landon settled both hands on her hips, tipped her chin up and gave Charlotte a long, hard look, as though she were secretly suspicious that Charlotte had been using Lady Denfield as a mere excuse. "I have told you before that you are to stay away from Lord Silverton."

"It is for the best that you do as asked. Your mother is doing all that she can to protect you."

Lady Florence's mother sent a warm smile toward Charlotte and then received a grateful look from Lady Landon.

"I am well aware that you have excellent intentions, Mama," Charlotte replied quietly. "Although will you not tell me specifically *why* I must stay far from him?"

Lady Landon shook her head firmly.

"There is no need for you to know. Believe me, I am saying this so that you are protected from any harm, and also so that rumors do not spread around London. You know full well that I am not inclined towards gossip, and I should not like to be the one to start something such as that."

Charlotte took in a deep breath and then nodded slowly. Her mother had always been disinclined towards gossip, and Charlotte had respected her for that. But now, at this present moment, she found herself a little irritated.

"Very well, Mama. Might I now take a turn about the room with Lady Florence??"

Lady Landon's eyes went over Charlotte's shoulder and a quick smile came to her lips.

"I do not think you will have the opportunity," she replied. "Look now. Lord Nettlesworth is coming to speak with you, Charlotte! Stand tall and make sure that you smile. He is an *excellent* gentleman and a good deal more suitable than Lord Silverton."

Thinking it best to be obedient, Charlotte turned

quickly, ready to greet Lord Nettlesworth, although in the back of her mind remained Lord Silverton and Lady Denfield, to the point that she could not help but cast a glance towards them. Her disappointment soared as she saw that they still stood close together, talking at length. Her dismay grew upon seeing Lord Silverton smile in a way that he had not done with her for some time. It seemed that her quiet remarks to Lady Denfield had made very little impact upon Lord Silverton, despite her belief to the contrary. Could it be that he was truly staying away from every eligible young lady in London? Or was it only that he had said such a thing to cover up the fact that he was staying far away from her alone?

CHAPTER SEVEN

"Good evening, Lord Silverton... again!"

Thomas' brows lifted in surprise as Lady Denfield approached him. This was the second time he had seen her in this one evening, given that he'd had two separate events to attend, one after the other. He had not expected to see her again so soon, however, and certainly had not thought that she would be seeking him out.

"Good evening to you also. I did not know that you were acquainted with Lord Huddersfield. "

The lady laughed, her eyes twinkling.

"In that, you would be correct. You are obviously aware that Lord Huddersfield is known to only keep *particular* company, thus I understand you might very well be surprised that a lady such as myself would be well acquainted with him."

A little embarrassed, Thomas quickly shook his head.

"That is not what I meant. I did not mean to insult you, I thought only–"

Lady Denfield put one hand on his arm, silencing him.

"I am not insulted, Lord Silverton. Pray do not concern yourself, I am only teasing you. My late husband was well acquainted with Lord Huddersfield, which is why, I assume, I have been invited to this particular evening."

A jolt of awareness reminded him that Lady Denfield was not the woman he had first believed her to be. Seeing the ring on her finger, he considered that she must still wear it to remember her late husband. Surely, he considered, if Lady Denfield still wore her late husband's ring some years after his death, he need not worry about his acquaintance with her. She obviously still cared very deeply for her late husband and thus, he could have no concern in speaking with her.

"I see." Clearing his throat, Thomas put both hands behind his back. "I am sorry to hear about your late husband. That must have been a very trying time indeed, especially given that you were not wed for long, I understand."

Something flickered in Lady Denfield's clear green eyes.

"You have been asking about me then?"

A gentle warmth began to form in Thomas' chest, rising up slowly into his face. There was a small smile playing about Lady Denfield's mouth and a softness in her eyes which took him a little by surprise. Was she attempting to tease him a little more? Or was she simply saying such a thing to avoid discussing her late husband?

"My friends saw that we had become acquainted, and we spoke a little of you, yes." It had only been a brief exchange, and only with Lord Pottinger and Lord Wiltsham, he reminded himself. The reason he had done so was because he had been a little concerned about her present situation, and his own circumstances. Given that he had promised himself he would stay away from all eligible ladies, the last thing he wanted to do was seek out a closeness between himself and Lady Denfield, when she was, in fact, eligible for marriage. In addition, he had caught a glimpse of Lady Charlotte glancing over at them when he had been enjoying a long conversation with Lady Denfield. The last thing he wanted was for Lady Charlotte to think that there was some connection between himself and the widowed lady. But when Lady Denfield came to speak to him, what could you do but talk with her?

"Is that so?"

A slight lift of her eyebrow sent flame shooting up into his face.

"But that is only because I was embarrassed at my lack of awareness as to your sad circumstances. I wanted to make certain that I did not display such foolishness again."

Lady Denfield tilted her head gently, her green eyes soft.

"There was no reason for you to know such a thing."

"Be that as it may, I was still a little embarrassed. I spoke to my friends about your situation so that I would have knowledge of it, and not prove myself a fool the next time we spoke."

It was one thing to know that she was widowed and, therefore, eligible, but he had to know for certain that the young woman was not seeking out a second husband for herself. Unfortunately, neither of his friends had been able to say much about Lady Denfield herself, nor her intentions.

"Well, that is good of you." There was a small, soft smile on Lady Denfield's features and her fingers brushed across his hand as she then ran them up his arm lightly for a moment. "You need not be so concerned, although it is very good of you to make certain that you know of my situation, without having to speak to me of it. I appreciate your consideration in that."

The brief touch was enough to make him start in surprise, but there was not any sort of warmth that came with that sensation. Rather, Thomas found himself thinking only of Lady Charlotte. He could not allow himself to have any feelings for Lady Denfield, could not allow himself to show any partiality towards her either. It would not be right, not after what he had promised. She would have to be just the same as every other person in London would be to him: spoken to briefly and infrequently, and keeping his distance as best he could.

"I should take my leave of you and allow many of the other gentlemen here to speak with you also, as I am certain that they are eager to do so."

Lady Denfield's eyes flared.

"You would not simply leave me, Lord Silverton? I do not know very many people at this occasion, I confess, since, as I have said, my husband was the one Lord Huddersfield was friends with."

A nudge of guilt pushed itself into Thomas' heart.

"I certainly shall not leave you alone." His thoughts scrambling, he concluded that he could introduce her to a few other people before taking his leave. He was all the more astonished when she tucked her arm into his and leaned a little against him, although her gaze held his for a few moments also. This was not moving back from her, this was not taking himself away from her. Instead, this was pushing him towards a closeness that he neither wanted nor desired.

What was he to do?

Clearing his throat, Thomas turned so that they faced

the other guests. A few tables had been set out, and soon games of cards would be played. Expecting the evening to be an excellent one, an evening where he might enjoy himself rather than think of his difficult and impoverished circumstances, he now felt very awkward indeed. He had never asked for Lady Denfield's closeness, but it appeared as though she was giving it to him, nonetheless.

Perhaps I can introduce her to some acquaintances and thereafter detach myself from her for good.

Taking quick, hasty steps, he came to a small group of gentlemen with two ladies also present. He made the introductions to those who did not know Lady Denfield and then expected to be able to step away, only for one of the other ladies to speak.

"I confess I am surprised to see you on the arm of Lord Silverton, Lady Denfield."

The remark was made by a young woman to whom Thomas had never before been introduced. He did not know her family, so why should she make such a remark as that? And with such obvious astonishment written in her expression? A streak of surprise rushed through him as he caught the way that the second lady nudged the first, mayhap urging her to stay silent, or demanding her silence for some other reason.

"I do not know what you mean." Lady Denfield shot the young lady a questioning look, but the young lady who had spoken simply shook her head, mute. Thomas' embarrassment burned. He had no knowledge of what the young lady meant but was a good deal insulted, nonetheless. Lifting his chin, he glared at her but, much to his astonishment, the young woman looked back at him with a hard gaze, as though *he* ought to be ashamed of himself. Lady Denfield broke the silence. "I think Lord Silverton is an excellent gentleman."

Rather than being embarrassed by Lady Denfield's defense of him, Thomas stood a little taller, finding himself glad of her support. He did not know what the young lady had meant by what she had said, for he had never treated any young woman in society cruelly in the past. Why should he do so now?

And then it came to him. Thus far, no one had mentioned his poverty. The *ton* had not spoken of it as yet, although he had been fully aware that whispers would no doubt be circulating. Why it had not been spoken of specifically, he could not say, but that, of course, was what this young lady meant. Why should he have Lady Denfield on his arm when he could not afford a wife? Shame rushed through him until the urge to stay away from the group grew so strong that he did precisely that. Muttering an excuse, he turned on his heel, taking Lady Denfield with him.

"Are you quite well, Lord Silverton?"

The concern in Lady Denfield's voice was a comfort. Shaking his head, he continued to walk to the other side of the room, eager to get away from the group.

"It must be difficult to hear something untoward being said of your character." Lady Denfield smiled softly when Thomas glanced toward her. "I do not know what that young lady meant but it did not sound very pleasant." For whatever reason, it was on the tip of his tongue to be honest, but instead, Thomas merely shrugged. "I cannot think that you are anything but an excellent gentleman." The warmth in Lady Denfield's voice brought the smallest of smiles to Thomas' features. "I am aware that we are only a little acquainted, but I pride myself on having the very best judgment about a person's character, once we are acquainted."

Thomas glanced at her.

"And what if your judgment is wrong?" Lady Denfield stopped suddenly. Her face went a little pale, her hand still on his arm but a slightly wide-eyed, frightened expression running across her features. "That is not to say that you are wrong, however," Thomas said quickly, realizing the cause of her fright. "I should not like to disabuse you of the notion of my good character. I am an excellent gentleman in every way, I assure you."

"Then what is the reason for Lady Willoughby's remarks about why I ought not to be on your arm?"

Again, Thomas fought the urge to tell her, only to remind himself that he did not know the young woman very well at all. This was, in fact, the first day of their meeting. Her defense of him had made him feel a little more warmly towards her than he otherwise would have done, certainly, but that did not mean that he ought not to guard his mouth.

"I do not know," he lied. "I appreciate your words in defense of me, however. It was most kind."

Her smile warmed his heart a little, chasing away some of the despair which threatened to grasp hold of his heart.

"But of course. As I have said, I am fully convinced that you are a more than amiable gentleman." She pressed his arm a little tighter. "Although you shall have to prove it to me so that I am not ashamed nor embarrassed in such a belief. That does mean that our acquaintance will have to continue."

All thought of keeping his acquaintance with Lady Denfield brief flew from his mind. She had defended him without even being fully aware of his character, and now trusted him when he had told her he was not a scoundrel.

Lady Willoughby's words were not meant to be a remark on his character, he knew, but more about his lack of funds – but at the present, he did not want to tell Lady Denfield about that.

"I am certain I shall be able to prove myself to you, of course."

"Good."

Her green eyes were vivid and clear as she smiled up at him, and Thomas' breath decided to curl in his chest at the sight of her. Lady Denfield was a very beautiful woman. He had no trouble in admitting that to himself, although reminding himself quietly that it could be nothing more than that... and then came a great flood of guilt as he recalled Lady Charlotte, remembering the sadness and confusion in her eyes when he had pushed her away. Mayhap he was being flattered by Lady Denfield's kind words, a lady who barely knew him, a lady who seemed to want to believe the best of him without knowing the truth. Who was she in comparison to Lady Charlotte? Lady Charlotte was someone he thought well of, someone he knew, who had come back to him repeatedly, even though he had injured her with his words. There had been a promise made to Lady Charlotte and he would keep his word to her so that he would not injure her any further. There was to be no close acquaintance between himself and Lady Denfield – there could not be, not when he had said such a thing to Lady Charlotte. To permit himself to become close would add further wounds to Lady Charlotte's already injured heart, and he had no desire to do such a thing.

"Are you both to play cards this evening?"

Thomas caught the glimmer of surprise in Lord Pottinger's expression as he came close to them. Ignoring it, he shrugged, then glanced towards the table.

"If it is only a game of cards and nothing more serious, then yes, I should be very glad to play."

Lord Pottinger let out that gruff laugh, clearly aware of what it was that Thomas meant.

"I quite agree." His gaze turned towards Lady Denfield. "And you?"

"I shall only be able to play if one of you fine gentlemen is able to sit with me to make certain that I do not make any ridiculous mistakes." Throwing one hand out towards the table, she let out a laugh. "I am afraid it has been some time since I have played any sort of game. During my mourning, I missed company and enjoyments such as this – and, indeed, only returned to London last Season. Even then, I did not play very many games of cards."

"I am certain that we will be able to oblige you."

Gesturing to a chair, Thomas helped Lady Denfield to sit down and then took a seat beside her, with Lord Pottinger on the other side. A good deal more satisfied, he smiled to himself. No longer was it just himself with Lady Denfield, there was also Lord Pottinger present. To his mind, he could both be obliging and kind but did not need to develop his acquaintance with the lady any further.

His smile quickly faded as, once more, Lady Charlotte's sad eyes rose in his mind. He hated that he had injured her so, and was upset with all that he had done. Would he ever be able to find a way to apologize? To tell her exactly what had happened, and how sorry he was for all of it? Or would this strange separation continue, without even a single word of explanation?

CHAPTER EIGHT

"He has spent the last fortnight in her company."

Lady Florence nodded.

"Yes, you are right. It is more than foolish of the gentleman to behave so, especially after what he said to you."

"I do not understand."

More irritated than upset, Charlotte shook her head just as Lord Silverton laughed at something Lady Denfield had said to him. These last two weeks she had allowed herself to watch Lord Silverton carefully, noting the company he kept and praying that what he had said to her that he would do was, indeed, what he then went on to do. Now, it seemed that Lord Silverton had been caught by one Lady Denfield. For whatever reason, her conversation and company were regularly sought after – not just by Lord Silverton, but by many a gentleman, but it was Lord Silverton that she saw the lady with the most.

"I do not mean to come to his defense, but I will state

that it is *always* Lady Denfield who approaches him, rather than the other way around."

Lady Florence spoke quietly, as though she were afraid that she would upset Charlotte still further by saying such a thing but, in fact, those words brought a little light to Charlotte's dark soul.

She bit her lip.

"I had not thought of such a thing."

Allowing her gaze to flick across to him again, she considered that statement for a moment, recalling that, yes, she had very often seen Lady Denfield make her way toward Lord Silverton rather than the other way around.

"Although," Lady Florence finished, "perhaps he could make more of an effort to stay away from the lady."

"That is fair," Charlotte murmured. "Certainly, he *could* do so."

"But for whatever reason, however, it seems as though he has no desire to."

Charlotte's lip curled.

"It is very difficult to simply move away from someone who has accosted you in the middle of a busy London street."

Lady Florence chuckled.

"It is hardly as though he has been accosted." Touching her arm, she smiled. "Come. Let us remove ourselves from the carriage and make sure that we go to the milliners, just as we had planned. Spying on Lord Silverton will do neither of us any good."

Charlotte wanted very much to stay in the carriage and continue watching Lord Silverton but, recognizing that her friend was right, she gestured for the door to be opened. Stepping down, she placed a smile on her face, just in case Lord Silverton should look in her direction and see her.

A quick glance toward him told her that he would not. He was much too busy speaking with Lady Denfield and the other gentleman who had come to join them.

"To the milliners and then, mayhap, the bookshop? I have heard that there is a new novel that I should very much like to read."

Aware that her friend was doing all she could to distract her from Lord Silverton, Charlotte dragged her eyes away.

"Certainly."

She had come to town to purchase one or two things from the milliners, but now she had no interest in choosing some ribbons or new gloves. Her mind was much too busy thinking of Lord Silverton and the young Lady Denfield. She was incredibly beautiful, charming, and was now eligible also.

Nudging her, Lady Florence gave her a quick smile.

"I understand that it is deeply frustrating and perhaps even confusing, given how Lord Silverton stated he would do one thing, only then to do another. But you must put him out of your mind for the present, else you will have wrinkles, and wrinkles will do nothing to aid you, not at such a young age." Giggling, Charlotte smiled. "And when you are old, they will speak of wisdom, I am sure, but for the moment, do try to smile – or at the very least, do not draw your eyebrows together so."

Trying to avoid marring her features, Charlotte forced her lips upwards, although she did not smile. Sighing, Lady Florence stepped into the milliners, taking Charlotte with her, before going to look at the gloves and thereafter at the ribbons. Charlotte followed her, but nothing took her interest. Sighing, she glanced at the window, but it took all of her strength not to go to it and look out to see whether or not Lady Denfield was still speaking with Lord Silverton.

These last two weeks Charlotte and Lord Silverton had shared some brief conversations, and yes, they had met on more than one occasion, but there had been nothing of note, nothing which she could consider an explanation for his current and ongoing separation from her. Her mother had said nothing and, try as she might, she could garner nothing from her acquaintances either.

"You do not want to purchase anything?"

Charlotte shook her head.

"I apologize for my disposition at present. I am aware I am a little sullen."

She gave her friend a wry smile, but Lady Florence simply smiled in return, clearly taking no offense.

"I can quite understand your reasons." Her smile brightened. "Allow me to pay for my purchases, and then we can make our way to the bookshop... and you shall be able to see for yourself whether or not Lady Denfield is still in conversation with Lord Silverton."

Charlotte tried to laugh, to pretend that this was nothing more than foolishness on her part, but did not refute the idea. Lady Florence's eyes twinkled, and she stepped away, going to purchase her items before returning to Charlotte. Making her way to the door, Charlotte stood in anticipation, her hands clenching tightly as she waited for Lady Florence to join her. The seconds seemed to tick by with infinite slowness, leaving her fighting for composure.

The moment that they stepped outside, however, her anticipation shattered. Lord Silverton was not there any longer, and Lady Denfield had also taken her leave, it seemed. There were a good many passersby, and certainly many gentlemen and ladies, but those two in particular were nowhere to be seen.

What if they went walking together?

"You see?" Lady Florence smiled and took Charlotte's arm. "There is no one here. No doubt Lord Silverton took his leave, and Lady Denfield went her way also."

Charlotte tried to smile but felt her heart sinking. Yes, she had said that she had wanted to see whether or not Lord Silverton was still conversing with Lady Denfield, but the truth was, she realized, that it was Lord Silverton she had wanted to see most of all. The fact that he was gone from here now meant that she had an ache in her heart. It was a heart that still yearned to be as closely acquainted with him as they had been before. There had never been anything said between them, of course, but that interest in him, that slight thrill that came to her heart whenever she laid eyes upon him, was still very much there.

"Yes, of course. The bookshop." Giving her friend a small smile, she pulled her eyes in the direction of the book shop. "We should make our way there, rather than stand lingering on the pavement, I suppose!"

Lady Florence laughed, and the sound pulled away some of Charlotte's upset. Managing to smile, she allowed her friend to lead her towards the bookshop, putting a gentle spring in her step and telling herself to stop being so very ridiculous. She had spent the last fortnight thinking of no one other than Lord Silverton, treasuring every glance in her direction, filled with happiness whenever he smiled at her. For her mother's benefit, of course, she did as she was asked, remaining far from Lord Silverton unless she had no other choice but to speak with him. However, she could not put him from her mind, even though she was meant to be doing that very thing. Instead, the further away she stayed, the more frequently he came into her thoughts, and the more eager she became to see him again. She had repeatedly reminded herself that this was simply because of the mystery that he presented, but the truth was that it was a little more than that.

"I do so like to be in a bookshop. It smells wonderful!" With a smile, Lady Florence stepped inside, and Charlotte followed her. "I shall go and speak with the man at the desk about that new novel I am seeking."

"Very well. I have nothing I wish to seek out at present." Gesturing to her left, Charlotte began to wander toward the many shelves of books. "I will be here, however, exploring the shelves. I may find something to capture my interest after all."

Throwing her a quick smile, Lady Florence turned her attention back towards the desk as Charlotte wandered along through the bookshop itself, enjoying the silence and letting the quiet calm her thoughts.

Picking up one book, she turned it over in her hands and then set it back without even so much as glancing inside. There was nothing that could capture her interest. She was not much of a reader, despite her mother's encouragement.

"It is all going well then."

"Yes, I believe so."

It took Charlotte a moment to realize that she was listening to a conversation between two people, who must be standing on the other side of the shelves that she was perusing. They were both speaking rather quietly, and she had not even been aware that they were present in the bookshop until this moment. Her face flushed as she thought of what they might say should they discover her nearby, afraid that they would think that she had been deliberately eavesdropping.

"Do you think that he is aware?"

"Aware of the situation?"

A quiet laugh trilled, and Charlotte's stomach dropped suddenly. She knew that laugh; she knew *exactly* who it was who was speaking, and her interest grew swiftly. Reminding herself that she ought not to be paying any attention to what was being said, given that she was not part of the conversation, Charlotte made to turn away, only for something more to catch her ears.

"Silverton has not come back to White's."

"Which is a relief, is it not? And I do not think that you can blame him, given that he believes that the *ton* know of his circumstances."

"Certainly, I do not throw any blame on him. In fact, I am rather glad, for it is to our advantage!"

Charlotte blinked rapidly, all the more confused by what was being said. What circumstances were they speaking of? Why was Lord Silverton unwilling to go to White's? And what advantage was this that this man spoke of?

"You are still taking something of a risk." The lady's voice softened, and Charlotte closed her eyes, quite certain now of who was speaking. "If he should set foot in White's, then we might *lose* that advantage. If his friends should discover it, then-"

"Pray do not concern yourself with that. If all is well, then all shall remain well. I have confidence."

"Charlotte?"

Charlotte's pulse quickened as she heard Lady Florence call softly for her. Desperately afraid that those speaking would discover that she had been near, she turned quickly, and, lifting her gown so that it would not rustle, hurried back towards the front of the shop.

"Ah, there you are. Have you found anything of note?"

Charlotte grasped her friend's hand.

"Please, do not ask me why, but we must take our leave at once."

Lady Florence blinked.

"I am waiting for my book. The man is only just now preparing it so that I might take it with me." Closing her eyes briefly, Charlotte let out a slow breath, trying to calm the frantic beating of her heart. The bookshop door opened and closed again, and this time a few other young ladies stepped inside. Looking at them all, Charlotte allowed her breath out again, feeling a good deal of relief that they were no longer the only two young ladies present in the bookshop. "Whatever is the matter?" Lady Florence's eyes were searching Charlotte's face for an answer, but she merely shook her head. There could be nothing said here, not when those present might still be watching her. Keeping her face turned towards the door, she gestured towards the desk.

"Look, I believe your book is ready."

Lady Florence blinked, frowned, but then turned back towards the man, who nodded. She went to fetch her book as Charlotte drummed her fingers on the shelf beside her, holding her breath as her friend picked up the book and paid for it. She dared not look over her shoulder for fear of whom she might see watching her. Perhaps she would be fortunate, and they would not know that she had been the one studying them. If she were found out, then everything could become rather awkward. She would have to explain why she had been eavesdropping while allowing her concern for Lord Silverton to grow continually. Thus far, she had very little understanding of what she had heard, only to know that there was something about Lord Silverton that was of great interest to those two who had been speaking.

Taking her arm, Lady Florence marched them both

towards the door. Once they stepped outside into the glorious sunshine, she opened her mouth to ask a question, but Charlotte gave her another swift shake of her head. They still could not speak, not until she was safely back in the carriage.

"Wait for a few moments longer, I beg you."

Lady Florence frowned but kept silent, much to Charlotte's relief. The carriage was not far away, and Charlotte practically scrambled inside, sitting down opposite her friend, and closing her eyes, resting her head back and blowing out a long breath.

"Goodness." Lady Florence's eyes widened. "Whatever is it that has happened?"

Opening her eyes, Charlotte let out another breath, aware of the bead of sweat which ran down her spine.

"I overheard someone speaking in the bookshop."

"I should reprimand you for eavesdropping," Lady Florence teased, but Charlotte was in no mood for mirth.

"They spoke of Lord Silverton."

In an instant, the smile shattered on Lady Florence's face. She sat forward, her hands clasping tightly in front of her, and her eyes fixed on Charlotte.

"Whatever do you mean?"

"I heard them speaking of Lord Silverton. I do not understand entirely what it was that they meant, but there was something about him, some scheme which involves him, of which he is unaware. I confess that I am no longer merely interested in the situation, I am now gravely concerned."

Lady Florence blinked, bit her lip, and then spread her hands.

"Mayhap it is a scheme that he is already aware of – are you certain that what they said indicated that he did not know? Perhaps we are concerned for nothing. You do not want to pry into a situation where he is already fully involved."

Charlotte shook her head, a lump in her throat as she gazed back at her friend.

"I do not think that he can be aware of this scheme, not given what was said," she said confidently. "I do not know who the gentleman was, who spoke, but I am certain of the lady's identity." Taking a breath, she looked straight into Lady Florence's face. "It was none other than Lady Denfield."

CHAPTER NINE

"You are looking at her again."

Thomas immediately turned his head away and shrugged.

"I am not looking at anyone in particular," he lied. "You know full well that I am doing nothing other than keeping my distance from every eligible lady, concentrating my efforts on Lord Montague and my fortune, although I must say that I am doing very poorly on that front."

"Again, I will remind you that it is not your fault that you cannot remember much." He put one hand on Thomas' shoulder for a moment. "You have been very kind in switching your attentions to Lord Montague rather than to your fortune."

A rueful grin spread across Thomas' face.

"And I have been a *great* help to you in that regard these last two weeks, have I not?"

Hearing his obvious sarcasm, Lord Foster chuckled.

"It is not as though *any* of us have had any success whatsoever." Grimacing, he turned his gaze towards Lady Foster, who was talking to Lady Wiltsham. "I confess I am a little embarrassed. I am now concerned that I did not, in fact, see Lord Montague in the carriage, just as my dear lady wife was so sure of. I have convinced you all that he has returned, only for none of our attempts to find him having any success."

Thomas shook his head.

"That does not mean that you were not correct, and I do not think that Lady Foster said you were wrong either. She said that you *may* have been mistaken, but your conviction was such that she did trust you."

"She is an excellent lady." Lord Foster sighed quietly, his eyes still on his wife. "She calms me when I am overwhelmed, she steadies me when I lurch from one side to the next."

Much to Thomas' surprise, jealousy ran straight through his heart, and he had to look away. The next person who came to mind was none other than Lady Charlotte, although he pushed all thought of her away almost as quickly as it arrived. He had done very well this last fortnight. He had managed to keep his distance from her, and although they had shared one or two conversations, they had been short. That was for the best. There could not be any connection between them, not when, no doubt, everyone in London knew of his circumstances. It was still a puzzle for him why no one had mentioned it as yet, but perhaps it was that none had the courage. Or mayhap, given that it was a rumor which circulated without his ears hearing it, the *ton* wanted to keep it that way, believing that it would either prove itself true or false in time.

"Are you thinking of Lady Denfield?"

Surprised, Thomas' gaze shot directly back towards his friend, his eyes widening.

"Am I thinking of Lady Denfield?" he repeated, quite

astonished that his friend would say such a thing. "Certainly, I am not. Why do you ask?"

Lord Foster shrugged.

"No particular reason." Lord Foster smiled, a slight redness in his cheeks. "It was more from the expression on your face. I thought that you would be thinking of a young lady, and the only person I considered was Lady Denfield, given that she has been spending some time with you of late."

Immediately Thomas shook his head.

"I have never approached her. She is always the one who comes to seek me out."

Lord Foster held up one hand in an expression of defense.

"I did not mean anything by it. She is an eligible lady, and I merely thought –"

"I have no feelings whatsoever." As he spoke, Thomas realized that he spoke the truth. He had no feelings for Lady Denfield. Yes, she was pleasant to talk with and certainly, she was very beautiful, but she did not strike a single jolt of interest in his heart. Aware of his friend's slightly disbelieving look, Thomas grew exasperated. "I was thinking of Lady Charlotte." At this, Lord Foster's eyebrows lifted even higher, and Thomas berated himself for speaking so hastily. "Which I should be refraining from, given that her mother has asked her to stay far from me and I have told her the same," he finished as Lord Foster kept his mouth shut, clearly unwilling to say a single word. "In fact, I should stop talking of her. I am not allowing myself to think of anyone."

"I must say that Lady Denfield is clearly delighted with your company." Ignoring what Thomas had just asked, Lord Foster continued to speak on the matter regardless. "You mean to say that you truly have no feelings for her in that regard?"

"I certainly do not."

Speaking with as much firmness as he could, Thomas glared at his friend, only for Lord Foster to chuckle, which in turn wiped the frown from Thomas' face. In fact, he could not help but grin back in return.

"She is a wealthy woman." Tipping his head, Lord Foster lifted one shoulder. "Could it be that she is seeking a husband for herself? Mayhap you are her chosen suitor?"

"Then I shall disabuse her of that notion immediately, should it come to it," Thomas replied firmly. "That will certainly not be a pleasant situation, but she cannot allow himself to think of me as a suitable husband."

"And should she ask you as to why?"

Thomas spread out both hands.

"Then I shall have no choice but to tell her the truth. A truth which I am quite surprised she does not know of as yet." His hands dropped to his sides. "Unless it is that she already knows of my impoverished circumstances and has been kind enough not to mention them, although I would question then why she is willing to remain in my company! Why she would consider me as a potential suitor, knowing that I am poor?"

Grinning, Lord Foster tipped his head.

"Perhaps she thinks you exceptionally handsome."

Laughing, Thomas opened his mouth to say more, only for someone to touch his fingers. Turning around, he saw, to his utter astonishment, that Lady Charlotte stood a little behind him. There was no color in her cheeks, her eyes were a little narrowed, and no smile was gracing her lips.

"Lady Charlotte" Looking around, Thomas frowned. "What are you –?"

"I must speak to you at once."

Blinking in surprise, Thomas took in Lady Charlotte's expression. Her hand was still pressed to his and her eyes were steely, as though by fixing him with her gaze, she would be able to express the fervency of her demands.

"My dear lady, we both know that this is not something that you are permitted to do. Indeed, I also discouraged you from speaking with me. Why do you persist?"

"Because I must."

Her fingers twisted through his and delicious warmth began to snake up his arm from that point of contact.

Still, however, he held himself back.

"I do not think that there is anything which can be of such seriousness that you should demand that I come away with you in the midst of a social occasion."

He was sure that this would be the end of the matter but, to his utter astonishment, Lady Charlotte simply turned on her heel and began walking away. Her fingers were still tight in his and Thomas found himself following her, regardless of his own desires. Yes, he could pull himself away but to do so might cause a slight commotion and he did not want to draw any unnecessary attention. His stomach turned over on itself as he suddenly began to wonder whether or not this was to do with his fortune - if she was determined to know, once and for all if it was true. If that were the case, then he would simply have to tell her the truth. She deserved that, at the very least.

"Lady Charlotte, where are you going?"

The house and the garden were very busy, given the number of guests who had been invited to the afternoon tea. Nonetheless, Lady Charlotte managed to find a quiet spot, stepping into the library where no other guests were present.

The moment the door was pushed to, fear crawled into Thomas' chest. They were almost entirely alone as the door was only ajar. Their hands were still joined, and with an exclamation, he pulled it back.

"You need not be concerned. I am here also."

A young lady stepped forward and Thomas turned to face her, barely recognizing Lady Florence, such was his astonishment at what was taking place

"I do not understand. Whatever is the meaning of this?"

Lady Charlotte dropped his hand and took a small step back. There was a frown pulling at her eyebrows and her eyes were a little narrowed.

"You thought that I was here to deliberately force your hand in some way? To trick you into marrying me?"

"I... I did not know what to think, but yes, that was my first thought."

Her frown grew heavier still.

"At least you are honest, but do you really think that I would be willing to do such a thing? You are mistaken! I would never behave in such a despicable manner."

A little embarrassed over his reaction, Thomas clasped his hands behind his back and nodded.

"Yes, I understand. I should not have thought ill of your intentions."

"No, you should not have. Especially when Lady Charlotte is doing what she can to protect you."

Lady Florence's gaze narrowed, and she held his, a slightly insolent look about her. All the more embarrassed, Thomas cleared his throat and returned his attention to Lady Charlotte. He said nothing more but waited for her to speak, to explain why it was that she had dragged him in here.

"I begged you to speak with me, because it is a matter of great urgency."

Moving a little closer, Lady Charlotte looked up into his face and immediately, all concern over his presence with her faded. How could he ever have doubted her sincerity? He knew that she was an honorable young lady and the chances of her lying to him were entirely non-existent.

"Then what is it?"

Wincing obviously at the rather gruff tone he had used, Thomas dropped both hands. He tried to say something further, but she was already speaking.

"It is about something I have overheard." A light pink came into her cheeks, but she continued speaking at a rapid pace. "It was not deliberate by any means. I was in the book-shop yesterday with Lady Florence and as I perused the books, I heard something which was not for my ears."

"If it was not for your ears, then I am surprised that you paid any attention."

At this, Lady Charlotte seemed to grow to twice her size, red with indignation. Standing as tall as she could, her eyes blazed with fury, and he suddenly felt incredibly small.

"Do not dare reprimand me! This is a situation of which you have no knowledge, and I am doing my very best to inform you of it, despite the fact that even speaking to you is going against my mother's wishes. I will find myself in a difficult situation should we be discovered, so pray, do not tell me what I should or should not have done, especially when I am doing all that I can to be of aid to you."

Thomas had never seen her behave so and the fact that she spoke with such vehemence took him aback. Yes, she was severe, but at the same time his consideration of Lady Charlotte grew significantly. She was almost majestic in her righteous anger, revealing the fierce and determined heart which lay within her.

Rather humbled, he spread his hands.

"Forgive me, Lady Charlotte, you are quite correct. I should not be saying anything about this situation which you found yourself in." Inclining his head, he lifted his gaze back towards her face and saw her slowly shrink back. Her shoulders dropped, but her head was still lifted, and her eyes held fast to his, glowing with her fierce resolve. "Tell me what it is that you were going to say."

"As I was saying." Lady Charlotte cleared her throat lightly, then threw a quick glance towards her friend, who gave her a small nod of encouragement. "I heard a conversation take place. A conversation about you."

In an instant, Thomas' heart beat hard and uneven, for he knew now exactly what was to come. There would be questions about his fortune, questions about his standing in society and he would have to tell her the truth about it all.

"What was it they were saying?"

Unwilling lips spoke such a question, but he could not simply stand there, mute. His eyes took in the frown which danced around her forehead, and his hands had tightened as he forced himself to remain calm, despite what was coming.

"Two people spoke of you. They thought you knew about some situation or other – they did not explain what it was – and the other said that she did not think so."

"Oh."

Relief blurred his vision for a moment, for this was not what he had expected. He had thought she would simply begin to talk about his impoverished situation, but now, he was floundering.

"Someone was speaking of White's, asking whether you had gone back there, and the other saying that thus far you had not. There was also a concern that, should you do so, they might lose the advantage."

"The advantage?"

Lady Charlotte shrugged.

"If you were to ask me what such things mean, I am afraid you will be left entirely disappointed. I have very little idea. However," she continued, her voice dropping a little and her eyes suddenly soft as she took a step closer to him. "To my mind, it did not sound as though these people had your best interests at the forefront of their minds. They do not want anything good for you, Lord Silverton. It seemed very much to be a scheme that would harm you." Tipping her head, she put both hands to her waist, her eyes suddenly moving over his face as though perhaps searching for a clue, although a clue as to what, Thomas did not know. "They said that you would not have gone to White's because of your situation. Might I ask what situation that is?"

Thomas rubbed one fist over his forehead, his thoughts turning around so quickly that he could not sort one from the other. This did not sound very plausible, but as yet he did not allow himself to believe that Lady Charlotte could ever tell mistruths. The story was much too intricate, which meant that every single word was true. His next question was why two such people would ever be interested in him. Why would they be speaking of him in such a way?

"They are correct to say that I have not returned to White's since I came back to London." Murmuring half to himself, Thomas ignored Lady Charlotte's question. "And that is apparently to their advantage?"

"Yes, that is precisely what I heard." Lady Charlotte nodded quickly. "Does any of what I have said make sense to you?"

Wishing that there was a way for him to say that, yes, he understood every word, Thomas was forced to shake his head.

"No, I do not understand. There is a lot here for me to think about but, as yet, I am entirely uncertain as to what any of it means." Shooting a quick glance towards Lady Florence, he then turned his attention back to Lady Charlotte. She was biting the edge of her lip, looking up at him with clear blue eyes which held a myriad of questions. He was relieved that she chose not to ask them all, one after the other. Letting out a breath, he twisted his mouth to one side for a few moments. "And you say that this was spoken in a bookshop?"

Lady Florence was the one who answered, giving him a description of where the bookshop was, and Thomas' eyebrows drew together suddenly.

"Why, I was only a few yards from there yesterday afternoon. I was speaking with Lady Denfield and a few other acquaintances."

He added this last part on quickly, not wanting Lady Charlotte to think that he was very often in Lady Denfield's company, even though he was quite certain that she was all too aware of just how frequently he stood with the lady.

A flush rose into Lady Charlotte's cheeks.

"I am aware of that. I saw you there."

Blinking, Thomas bit back his next question, aware of the warmth in his own face. To know that Lady Charlotte had been near him, had been watching him, brought him both embarrassment and happiness. Embarrassment that he had not noticed her, but gladness too that *she* was still very much aware of him, even though, at this point, he felt as though he did not deserve a single thought from her. Her kindness in speaking to him about what she had heard showed both concern and consideration. He merited neither of those things from her, not after how he had distanced himself without explanation. It spoke well of her heart, and of her character, and Thomas had to resist the urge to move closer, to take her hand and press it. No matter how he wished to do so, he could not.

"I fear that I may upset you greatly with this next point." Licking her lips, Lady Charlotte threw a glance toward her friend before moving across the room to stand beside her. "There were two people speaking yesterday afternoon, one gentleman and one lady. I admit that I did not see their faces, but I am quite certain that I know who the lady in question was."

"Please." Unable to stop himself, Thomas moved closer, reaching to grasp her hand for a brief moment – although only by way of encouragement, he told himself. "Do not keep it from me. Do not fear to tell me, I must know who it is."

Lady Charlotte's hand was still in his. Her gaze was steady, but her face now a little pale.

"To remind you, I did not see their faces." Taking a breath, she licked her lips. "I am convinced that the voice I heard, the laugh which rang around the room, and what I listened to, came from the mouth of Lady Denfield." Thomas stared at her for some moments, unable to say a single word. Part of him wanted to laugh at the ridiculousness of the suggestion, but the other part told him that he had to take everything which had been said with a great seriousness. Lady Charlotte stared back at him, her audible breath quickening, it being the only sound that echoed through the room. Thomas swallowed, going hot all over. He was not going to, could not, tell her that she was wrong but yet, his mind did not want to believe it. "You... You have not said anything for some time."

Lady Charlotte pressed his hand, but Thomas immediately pulled his away.

"I do not understand what this means."

"I do not know either." Lady Charlotte took a small step back and flung her hands wide. "But I confess that I am concerned. Whatever they were speaking of, it did not sound at all good."

Thomas dragged air into his aching lungs, for the shock of what he had been told had not yet passed, and he did not seem to be able to think clearly.

"Perhaps we should leave Lord Silverton for the moment."

Lady Florence drew near and took Lady Charlotte's arm, but Thomas quickly shook his head.

"I am quite all right. I am just a little... overwhelmed with surprise. I do not know what I ought to make of all of this. Lady Denfield has been..." Coughing lightly, Lady Charlotte turned her head and a flame lit up Thomas' cheeks. "She has been staying close to me of late." Choosing to be honest, he simply continued to speak openly. "You are saying now that she is doing so for her own advantage, although as yet it is difficult to state exactly what that advantage could be."

She nodded.

"That is precisely what I am saying. I do not know what it is that you wish to do therefore, I shall leave that to you for the time being."

Despite his confusion, a small smile lifted one side of Thomas' mouth.

"I am afraid I do not think I can believe that, Lady Charlotte."

Her eyes flew wide, looking back up at him.

"I do not understand what you mean."

"Given the fact that you have not stayed far from me, despite the fact that your mother and I have both stated that it would be best for you to do so, I cannot believe that you are so easily willing to leave this matter with me."

Lady Charlotte blinked, and it took some moments for her to respond. However, much to Thomas' relief, she eventually smiled at him, a gentleness about her eyes that had not been there since they first set foot in the library.

"If you are asking me whether or not I will assist you in this matter, then the answer, of course, is yes."

She tipped her head gently, the smile remaining, and Thomas could not help but grin.

"I think you quite precocious, Lady Charlotte."

His smile faded as he spoke, realizing just what Lady Charlotte had brought to him.

Lady Florence took a step forward, grasping his attention.

"I do hope you understand how much of a risk Lady Charlotte has taken – not only taking you into this room but speaking to you so openly." One eyebrow lifted. "She has been greatly concerned for you."

Indeed, she has taken a chance in speaking to me, for she would not have known of my reaction.

Nodding slowly, Thomas turned his gaze back towards Lady Charlotte, who was watching him still. She said nothing, but he took her hand and, bowing over it, allowed his lips to briefly press against her skin. His ears caught the sound of her gasp, and he lifted his head quickly, seeing the flush rise in her cheeks as she turned her head away.

"I am truly grateful." Speaking honestly, he put one hand to his heart, releasing her hand with the other. "I shall think a great deal on what you have told me. If it is Lady Denfield, then I must reconsider my acquaintance with her. I must wonder who it is that she was speaking with and what their purpose was – or is – for me."

Lady Charlotte nodded and then turned her head back towards him, although for whatever reason she could not quite seem to meet his gaze.

"I will do what I can. I will continue listening, for I am able to be unobserved when I need to be. After all, who would pay attention to two young ladies who walk together as often as we do?"

She slid a gaze towards Lady Florence, who nodded fervently before reaching to take Lady Charlotte's arm.

"And speaking of such a thing, we must take our leave." Lady Florence urged. "We do not want your mother to have missed us."

"No indeed."

Giving him a quick smile, Lady Charlotte began to make her way toward the door. Thomas followed her with his eyes, wanting to say something more to her, wanting to find another way to express his gratitude, and his promise that he would truly continue to think about what she had told him, but no words came. Instead, as she turned to the door, her head swiveled back in his direction and their eyes met – and held – for a long moment. His heart dropped to his stomach, swirled around, and then shot back towards his chest, making him catch his breath. Lady Charlotte smiled, as though she knew exactly what it was that he was feeling, and then the door was closed and she was gone from him.

Closing his eyes, Thomas dropped his head and pushed one hand through his hair, letting the palm of his hand rest lightly against his forehead. So many emotions whirled around him that he could not comprehend what exactly it was he was feeling. Question after question poured into his mind. Was Lady Denfield in collaboration with another gentleman over some circumstance to do with him? Was that why she had been so close to him these last few weeks, given that they had never been acquainted before, why would she do such a thing as that?

It came to him that he had no doubt that everything which Lady Charlotte had said was true. That thought intrigued him and he smiled quietly to himself. There had been such a desperation in her voice, and such an eagerness in her eyes, that he could not doubt her, not even for a moment. She had taken a risk in coming to speak to him, and his gratitude was overwhelming. No longer could he deny that the single touch of his lips to her hand had sent fire into his blood. No longer would he push away the awareness that looking into her eyes was the only thing he wished to do. To stand close to her and to converse with her would bring such joy that he wanted to take hold of every opportunity he had to do it.

And perhaps now I will be given the opportunity, even though we must be cautious.

Taking a breath, Thomas lifted his head, dropped his hands, and went to the door. The first thing he would have to do would be to share this news with his friends and, thereafter, decide exactly what it was he was to do about Lady Denfield.

CHAPTER TEN

"You cannot keep staring at Lady Denfield."

Charlotte tossed her head.

"I am not looking at her!" Her face heated as her friend laughed. "I am waiting for Lord Silverton to arrive. That is why I keep looking around me."

The truth was that, while she *had* been looking for Lord Silverton, she was also looking at Lady Denfield. As yet, she was uncertain of whether or not Lord Silverton would take what she had told him with any great seriousness. The fact of the matter was that he could easily turn around and say that he did not believe her, or that the matter was of very little interest, and that the truth would out itself, soon enough, rather than do what *she* thought he ought to do, which was to find out the truth before it was too late.

"I am sure that Lord Silverton will be glad to talk to you, although will you still have to remain discreet?"

Charlotte nodded, but said nothing, all too aware that she would have to remain quite hidden from her mother. Her heart quickened a little as she saw Lady Denfield moving across the room. She herself had lingered near the door of the ballroom, wanting desperately to see the lady in question, as though by watching her, she might somehow ascertain exactly what it was that she was doing. It was a foolish thought, of course, but it was one which would not leave her. It was as if she felt obliged to do something for fear that Lord Silverton would not.

"You *do* have some feelings for Lord Silverton, then."

Lady Florence's voice was soft, and Charlotte fought to find a response that would not require her to be so brutally honest. Lady Florence chuckled.

"If you are thinking of pretending, then you need not do so. Have I not always encouraged you to think of your feelings when it comes to considering the gentlemen of London? I am glad now that you are doing so."

"I am concerned for him, that is all."

Not quite able to look at her friend, Charlotte managed a vague smile in Lady Florence's direction, but it was not enough to convince her.

"I do not believe that you would have acted in such a decisive manner if you had not had any true feelings for the gentleman." Lady Florence tipped her head, her gaze fixed on Charlotte's. "And you need not pretend either. I am delighted!"

Twisting her lips, Charlotte fought for an answer, but, in the end, did not give one. The truth was that her feelings for Lord Silverton had become very strange indeed these last few days. It was as though, in admitting to herself that she liked the gentleman, she had opened up her heart completely. The way that he had taken her hand when they had spoken had sent her heart into flurries, and the softness about his gaze had reached into her completely. For the present, she was trying to determine whether or not these feelings meant anything of significance, telling herself that she was only doing what she could for Lord Silverton, out of concern for him. In essence, she was trying to treat him as though he was just another gentleman, another one of her acquaintances, for whom she felt very little other than friendship - but with Lady Florence as her friend, she could not do such a thing. She could not merely pretend, not when her heart was already beginning to become involved.

"Look."

Her hand grasped her friend's arm tightly. Lord Silverton had just made his way into the room and within only a few moments of his arrival, Lady Denfield began to make her way quickly to his side. Charlotte's heart dropped to the floor when Lord Silverton smiled warmly at Lady Denfield, bowing over her hand. Whatever was he doing? Was this evidence that he had not taken Charlotte's concerns seriously?

"He does appear to be very cordial with her at present," she murmured as Lady Florence lifted one shoulder in a careless shrug.

"I do not think that need give you any concern." Lady Florence smiled. "You need not look so upset. Think about this! It is not as though Lord Silverton could say anything to the lady as yet, not when he is unsure – as we both are – of what exactly is going on. It is in his interest to keep a friendship between them for the present, as much as you may not like it."

This rang true, and Charlotte gave her friend a brief smile.

"I suppose that you are right." Charlotte laughed and immediately, her spirits lifted, despite the fact that Lord

Silverton and Lady Denfield were smiling warmly at each other. "Yes, you are right. It is as though my feelings for the gentleman have suddenly become exposed, simply from talking with him!" She lifted one shoulder. "Mayhap it has come from finding our separation to be no longer as... separate."

Lady Florence's eyes widened.

"I do not think that you will have to watch this situation for much longer. It appears as though Lord Silverton and Lady Denfield are walking together... and they are walking towards us."

Turning her head, Charlotte glanced towards Lord Silverton. His eyes darted towards her frequently, but he did not make any grand appearance of noticing her, and for that, Charlotte was thankful. Her mother was still somewhere nearby, and her father also, although he was most likely already playing cards. Her separation from Lord Silverton had only just begun to come to a close, and the last thing she needed was for her mother to put an end to it all over again.

Lady Denfield was paying very little attention to anyone, given the way that her eyes swiveled around the room, not looking at anyone in particular. So nonchalant was Lord Silverton that it seemed almost a surprise when he eventually greeted both Charlotte and Lady Florence.

"Good evening." He smiled and bowed as Lady Denfield murmured the same. "A pleasant soiree, is it not?"

"It is, and I have heard that there is to be some wonderful entertainment later this evening."

Charlotte smiled at them both, giving a sidelong glance to Lord Silverton. Whatever was his intention? Why had he come to speak to her so, especially with Lady Denfield on his arm?

"I am to play the pianoforte." Lady Florence spoke in a warm tone. "That is not to say that I am particularly distinguished but more that I am merely one of those who will be performing this evening."

Lord Silverton smiled, and it lifted the color in his eyes a little.

"I am certain that you do yourself a disservice. I look forward to hearing you play."

"As do I." Lady Denfield's smile was warm, and Charlotte suddenly felt rather guilty over her suspicion. What if the conversation she had overheard was nothing but a triviality? It certainly had not sounded like one, but then again, to make any sort of assumption about Lady Denfield's true intentions might make her look like a fool once the truth was discovered. The lady in question then smiled toward Charlotte. "And do you play the pianoforte also?"

Before she could prevent herself, Charlotte laughed, causing Lady Denfield's eyes to widen and even Lord Silverton to chuckle.

"I believe that would be a very firm no, Lady Denfield." Lord Silverton grinned. "I take it that you do not play, then, Lady Charlotte?"

"Alas, I do not. I am aware that it is generally a requirement for every young lady to be able to do so, but my mother, I am afraid, has given up on attempting to teach me. I think that she tried five different tutors before deciding that it would not work. "

Lady Denfield nodded and smiled as though she understood, although Charlotte was quite certain that she would be able to play the pianoforte very well.

"I am certain that you have many other talents. What hobbies do you enjoy?"

Charlotte was about to answer, only to catch Lord

Silverton's quick look. She ducked her head as though still considering, glancing at him again and seeing a small nod, his eyes flaring as though he were trying to tell her something without using any words. Praying that she was doing as he expected, she smiled.

"My mother is always telling me that I ought to be a great reader, but alas, I even fail her in that! Only a few days ago, Lady Florence and I made our way to one of the bookshops where my dear friend spent a long time in search of one particular book. Alas, I found the entire outing of very little interest to me."

"I can attest to the fact that Lady Charlotte's displeasure was quite true." Lady, Florence laughed. "I have tried so often to tell her that there are many great pleasures to be found in books, but she does not seem willing to give my words of wisdom any consideration."

Charlotte shook her head in mock dismay.

"I am sure that you will think me quite dreadful, Lady Denfield. Tell me, do you enjoy reading? Would *you* be much more inclined to stay in a bookshop with Lady Florence?"

She kept her voice light and a smile on her face whilst inwardly, every part of her buzzed with excitement as she waited to hear what the lady would say.

"I think that, when I was younger, I enjoyed reading a good deal more than I do at present." Lady Denfield smiled as though she had no concern whatsoever in speaking so. "I cannot recall the last time I was in a bookshop, however. I fear that while my interest in books is a little greater than yours, Lady Charlotte, it is a good deal *less* than yours, Lady Florence."

At this Charlotte glanced towards Lord Silverton, catching the slight frown on his face. Taking a breath, he made to say something, then shook his head, opened his mouth again, only to turn his head in clear confusion – to the point that even Lady Denfield noticed. Waiting for him to say whatever it was he wanted, Charlotte allowed silence to fall, looking from Lord Silverton to Lady Denfield and back again.

"Is there something wrong, Lord Silverton?" Obviously aware that there was something on Lord Silverton's mind, Lady Denfield touched his arm, her green eyes wide with obvious and expressive concern. "You look a little troubled."

Lord Silverton shook his head.

"It is nothing. I must have been mistaken."

Allowing her eyes to widen a little. Charlotte looked from one to the other.

"Pray, what is it? It is not something I have said, I hope."

Lord Silverton shook his head.

"No, it is not something that *you* have said."

The emphasis on this caused Lady Denfield's eyes to flare, and again her hand went to his arm.

"I have said something to confuse you." She moved a little closer, so that her nearness to Lord Silverton was increased all the more. "Pray, what is it?"

Sighing heavily, Lord Silverton shrugged, his mouth twisting for a second.

"It is only...."

There was a breath of silence, and even Charlotte felt as though she could not wait another moment to hear what it was that he had to say. It took all of her strength not to speak out encouragingly, and she let out her breath slowly when Lord Silverton began to speak.

"It is only that I was sure that I saw you departing from a bookshop only two days ago."

Lady Denfield's hand lifted immediately, pressing

lightly against her heart, her eyes going wider still as she drew back from Lord Silverton a little.

"Good gracious, Lord Silverton!" she gasped, as though he had done some great evil in stating what he had seen. "You do not think that I would ever lie to you about such a thing, do you? Why would I do so?" Charlotte blinked quickly, attempting to find an excuse that she might have been able to offer Lord Silverton. To his credit, however, Lord Silverton said nothing and, instead, merely allowed Lady Denfield to continue in her indignation. "You must have been confused, Lord Silverton. I would never have made up such a mistruth, especially over something as simple as this! You *must* have mistaken me for someone else."

With interest, Charlotte noticed how Lady Denfield's cheeks had gone a very pretty shade of pink, her eyes vivid with a clear and focused determination to have Lord Silverton believe her. Her stance was a little angry, however, with her hands at her waist, her elbows jutting out, and the slight tilt of her chin spoke of fury.

"I suppose that you are right." Lord Silverton's voice was quiet, his slight shrug of his shoulders seeming to calm Lady Denfield a little, although he did not either look or sound entirely convinced. Lady Denfield dropped her hands as Lord Silverton rubbed at his chin, looking at her thoughtfully as though he could somehow thereby ascertain whether or not she spoke the truth. "I confess that I am surprised to hear that I was mistaken. We had only just been talking and I was sure that the person I saw emerging from the bookshop as I made my way back towards my waiting carriage was none other than you."

At this, Lady Denfield's face turned scarlet.

"I am surprised to hear that you were still present, given

that you had stated that you were to return home at the very next moment! It should not matter if I made my way to another –"

She stopped short before she could say anything more. Charlotte's heart quickened, but she said nothing, wondering silently what it was that Lady Denfield had been about to say. At Lord Silverton's silence, she let her gaze drift towards him, all the more astonished by the thunderous expression he wore. His eyes had darkened, and his arms were now crossed over his chest. The air seemed to go thick with tension, and Charlotte shared a glance with Lady Florence. Her friend was staring at Lady Denfield and did not so much as even look at Charlotte. Whatever was going on at present was clearly very significant indeed.

"As I have said, I have not been in a bookshop for quite a long time," Lady Denfield's smile flickered, but her eyes did nothing other than fix on Lord Silverton as if silently begging him to trust her. Given that she had no real knowledge of the depths of Lord Silverton and Lady Denfield's acquaintance, Charlotte had no other choice but to stand in silence, looking first at Lady Denfield, and then towards Lord Silverton. He was still frowning, but shrugged, as though he were to accept Lady Denfield's explanation.

"Very well, Lady Denfield." His smile was tight. "I am mistaken."

Lady Denfield let out a small sigh.

"Thank you, Lord Silverton. Now, I think, I shall take my leave." Dropping into a bob that was barely a curtsey, she glanced at Lord Silverton then sent a small but cool smile in Charlotte's direction. "Do excuse me. I hope that you enjoy the rest of the evening, should we not have another opportunity to talk."

Murmuring something indistinct, but which sounded

friendly, Charlotte pressed one hand lightly to her stomach in an attempt to stop the swirling nervousness there and watched Lady Denfield as she walked away from the three of them.

"Goodness." Lady Florence clicked her tongue. "That was a little abrupt, was it not?"

"Do you believe her?" Charlotte spoke quietly, her gaze still on the retreating Lady Denfield. "When she said that she was not in the bookshop, do you think that she was telling the truth?"

"No, I do not think that she was truthful." Lord Silverton shot her a wry smile. "Thank you for being so very aware, Lady Charlotte. You understood what I wanted, what I hoped for from you, and walked into it beautifully."

His smile sent Charlotte's heart lifting, warming in a most overwhelming manner. Yes, there was still a gap to be closed between them, a good deal still to be explained, but at the present moment, Charlotte found herself suddenly very contented with the situation. It was a good deal better than being separated from him without explanation.

"This was a test." Lady Florence spoke confidently, tipping her head to one side. "To see whether or not she would tell you the truth about the bookshop."

"Which we now know she did not."

"Which is to my advantage," Lord Silverton remarked. "I wanted to speak about the bookshop in such a way that she would not become suspicious over my questions, thinking that I had seen her in there myself. This presented me with an excellent opportunity, an opportunity for me to tell her that I had been sure I had seen her leaving the shop, even though obviously, I did nothing of the sort."

"And it protects Lady Charlotte also."

Charlotte started in surprise, looking from Lady Florence to Lord Silverton. She had not considered such a thing. Lord Silverton could have simply stated that Charlotte had been the one to see Lady Denfield in the bookshop, but instead, he had simply said that *he* had been the one to take note of her. That had kept Charlotte from Lady Denfield's anger, although she did not like the fact that it was also directed towards Lord Silverton.

"I do not think that Lady Denfield was very pleased with your questions. She wanted you to believe that she was speaking the truth, and seemed very insulted when you suggested otherwise."

To Charlotte's astonishment, Lord Silverton simply shrugged, as though such a thing was of very little importance. Perhaps his consideration of the lady had been less than what she had at first thought. Did she dare believe it?

"I must know the truth." Lord Silverton gave a wry smile. "If Lady Denfield was the one in the bookshop speaking with this gentleman, then I needed to find a way to confirm it. I believe now that I have done so."

"Even though she stated that she had not set foot in that place?"

Lord Silverton chuckled, although it did not bring any light into his eyes.

"It was because of her vehemence, because of the color in her face, as well as the way that she would not look into my eyes, that I became convinced that she was not telling me the truth. Her words of honesty are void. My heart believes that Lady Denfield *is*, in fact, involved in some situation or other where I am the target."

Charlotte blinked.

"And what is it that you intend to do now?"

At her question, Lord Silverton hesitated. His eyes drifted across the room before returning to her, and when he smiled, Charlotte's heart threw itself toward the ceiling. There was a tenderness in that smile that she had never seen before, and the softness in his gaze told her that no matter what happened, she had nothing to fear. The separation between them now was at an end. He had not said those words out loud, but they were now standing on the cusp of a strange situation, and to untwist the threads of it, they would need to work alongside each other. That meant that she would very often be in his company, regardless of what her mother believed. She did not want to push him away any longer.

"I will consult my friends and, thereafter, make my way to White's, given that is where I am not meant to go, according to Lady Denfield and whatever gentleman she was speaking with."

The tenderness in his smile clasped itself around Charlotte's heart. The transformation in his manner and expression was quite astonishing, but also quite wonderful.

"I am uncertain of what I will discover there, but be assured that, whatever I learn, I will share that information with you, Lady Charlotte. You were right to come to me, and I appreciate that consideration a great deal. Otherwise, I would have continued my acquaintance with Lady Denfield, unaware of her other intentions... whatever they may be."

His smile slipped and his eyes pulled away, and before she knew what she was doing, Charlotte took his hand in hers. The shock of her action had his gaze slipping back towards her, and Charlotte fought to know what to say, eager to say something, but finding no words waiting on her lips.

And then his fingers curled around hers. A smile lifted the corners of his mouth as a blush rose on Charlotte's face. She could not say anything, and it was not until Lady Florence cleared her throat that the whirlwind of emotion finally blew itself away.

"I am afraid that we will only be able to meet in quiet corners and the like." Seemingly unwillingly to let go of her hand, Lord Silverton squeezed her fingers and then, with a sign, dropped her hand. "Your mother will still not want you near me, I am sure."

Keeping her gaze steady, Charlotte tipped her head to one side.

"And why might that be?" She spoke softly, and Lord Silverton shook his head. Charlotte was not willing to accept that dismissal, so she spoke again, this time with a good deal more urgency. "I know that there is something more. Why is it that you cannot tell me the truth? After all that has happened to you, do you truly believe that I would still push you away, should something be made known to me? I am already aware that it cannot be to do with your character, given that my mother has assured me that there is nothing of a defect in that regard. Why, then, can you simply not be honest? It is all so very strange, and I confess myself to be very frustrated indeed."

Lord Silverton dropped his head forward and then pushed one hand through his hair. As he did so, a sorrowful look pulled at the corners of his mouth and for some moments he simply stared at the floor. At the next, however, he lifted his head and looked straight at her.

"It is because I have no fortune." Astonishment rattled through her chest, making the breath still in her chest, her tongue sticking to her mouth as she stared at him. "You see? You are greatly shocked, are you not?"

Charlotte closed her eyes. However had such a thing occurred? The last that she knew of, Lord Silverton had been a very rich fellow indeed. He had been known to the *ton* as a most eligible gentleman with an excellent fortune; a man who need not care for anything, who had no concerns. Her eyes filling, she looked back at him, her vision blurring.

"That is why your mother did not want you to be close to me, I am sure. Because I cannot offer you a future."

"Then you... you have no coin because you have lost it all?"

Lord Silverton immediately shook his head.

"I am not as foolish as you might believe, Lady Charlotte. I have not been hiding my idiocy from you. The truth is, it was not offered as a bribe or in a game of cards. Rather, it was stolen, through wily ways and evil deeds. My fortune was *taken* from me. I have prayed that the *ton* might not become aware of it until I have had the opportunity to recover it, but I am certain that the truth has become known. That will be why your mother has begged you to stay away from me."

Charlotte blinked rapidly, pushing away the tears which lodged in her eyes, finding a lump beginning to form in her throat as she battled her emotions. She could not grasp what he meant, could not understand how a gentleman such as he would be able to lose his own fortune. How could it be stolen from him? How could he be unaware of it being taken from him? It was a question she could not answer, and as she looked up at Lord Silverton, she caught the desperation shining in his eyes, as though he could not wait a moment longer to know whether or not she would believe him.

"There is more to say, but perhaps now was not the time to say it."

Twisting his head around, he quickly lifted an eyebrow in Charlotte's direction and, as she looked, she caught sight of her mother. As yet, however, Lady Landon had not noticed them, but surprise and concern caught in her chest, nonetheless.

"For what it is worth, Lord Silverton, I have not heard any such rumors." Lady Florence was at Charlotte's side, her arm looping through hers again as she looked up at the gentleman. "You can be assured that neither myself nor Lady Charlotte will say anything to those who might gossip about such a situation, however. What you have told us will remain in our minds only."

Lord Silverton nodded, but Charlotte barely managed to look up at him again. Battling confusion over what had just taken place, she dragged in some air and then let it out again slowly. The situation was very confusing indeed, and she had a good deal to think about. Making to step away, she found Lord Silverton catching her fingers again, although he did not hold them for long, simply waiting for her to look back at him with any sort of response.

"You will speak with me again, will you not?"

The pain in his eyes made her heart sore, and, taking a breath, she broke through her confusion to give him a small smile.

"Yes, Lord Silverton. I should like to speak to you again very much. There's a good deal that I wish to understand."

"I would be glad to share it with you, for that is my desire also, Lady Charlotte." He inclined his head, his expression still grave. "Good evening."

Her eyes held his for a long moment before, finally, she nodded and then stepped away without a word. So much had been revealed in this one evening that she found herself quite astonished and, in truth, a little overwhelmed with the many things which had been told to her – as well as the vast amount that she did not yet understand. Some of what Lord Silverton had told her was incomprehensible, and yet she did not doubt that what he had said was the truth.

I will speak to him again very soon, she vowed silently. *And I will seek to understand it all.*

CHAPTER ELEVEN

"*I* believe that everything Lady Charlotte said was true."

Looking around the room, he took in the faces of his friends. They were all present, with Lady Foster and Lady Wiltsham also joining them. Some were wide-eyed in apparent astonishment, while some were frowning hard in either displeasure or uncertainty. Lord Foster, however, rose quietly from his chair, his hands clasping at his back and lines revealing themselves across his forehead as he began to pace up and down the room.

"Then she is attempting to do.... What, exactly?"

Thomas shrugged.

"I do not know. All I can tell is that she and this other gentleman are seeking to injure me in some way and are relieved that I have not yet visited White's." Shrugging, he spread out both hands. "But that should not be a grave concern of yours, Foster. I know that we must consider only Lord Montague at present, just as I have promised."

Lord Foster let out an exclamation.

"Do not concern yourself with that! We have all been

looking for Lord Montague and none of us have seen hide nor hair of him." He shook his head. "I am beginning to think that I was quite mistaken. What Lady Charlotte has told you, however, is much more important and significant - for that, at least, can be verified!"

"Foster, I–"

"Of course, you *must* focus your time on this. I understand that completely," Lord Foster continued. "And indeed, we urge you to look at this matter with all seriousness. There is clearly another motivation for Lady Denfield's acquaintance with you. You must discover what that purpose is, certainly."

Sitting forward in his chair, Lord Pottinger suddenly spread his hands so that his elbows rested on his knees, and his hands were flung out wide.

"Mayhap you will find out something about your fortune from this. Could it be that she was involved in some way?"

This was not something that Thomas had considered. Now that he did, however, his first thought was to doubt it.

"I would be very surprised indeed if she was. What could her motivation be for lingering close to me at this present moment if she already has my fortune?"

Lady Wiltsham and Lady Foster exchanged a look before one of them spoke. Their eyes were heavy, and no smile flickered across their faces, making Thomas' heart twist with a sudden flurry of nervousness.

"One possible motivation could be that she wishes to see you fall." Lady Wiltsham smiled apologetically. "It is not a kind consideration, I understand, but it is one that you might think of. Perhaps she knows of your particular circumstances and has such a depth of cruelty in her that, for whatever reason, she wishes to be the one to declare it to society. Mayhap she is waiting for you to ask to court her, only for her then to decry you to the entirety of the *ton*."

It was a most discomforting thought, and Thomas shifted uncomfortably. He did not want to even think of Lady Denfield having such cruelty about her, but then again, he truly did not know the lady. Yes, she had become more closely acquainted with him these last few weeks, but her motivation for doing so was something he could certainly question. He could not even begin to guess why Lady Denfield was treating him so.

"What is your first thought?" Lord Thornbridge asked. "How will you go about finding what Lady Denfield intends to do?"

A rueful smile spread across Thomas' face and embarrassment grew within him like a fire as he recalled the last time that he had been in White's with Lord Thornbridge.

"My first thought was that I should go to White's. Given that, whoever this gentleman was, believed that it would be to their disadvantage if I was to attend, that seems to be the most reasonable place to begin." Glancing around the room, he looked at each of his friends. "Have any of you been there of late?"

Each of them shook their heads.

"We have been much too busy." Lord Stoneleigh shrugged his shoulders as the others nodded. "There has always been something to do, someone to speak to, or something to investigate."

Thomas looked around the room again, a faint hope beginning to build.

"Would some of you be willing to accompany me to White's, then?"

Lord Pottinger chuckled.

"It is not as though we will be doing you some great and

distressing favor," he laughed. "In fact, I find myself quite looking forward to the prospect."

The others in the room also smiled and laughed as Thomas let out a hearty bellow. The sound seemed to astonish him, for it snapped away almost as soon as it had begun, and he found himself quiet and still. It surprised him because he had not laughed in so long. Being able to laugh was all because of Lady Charlotte, he realized. This was all because she had been willing to tell him of what she had overheard, convinced that it was Lady Denfield who had been talking of him in such a manner. Had she not done so, then he would be still quite in the dark. *She* was the one who had given him some hope, the one who had allowed him to smile and laugh again. He had very little idea of what he would discover in White's, but he was becoming increasingly more intrigued about what he might find out. Something would have to reveal itself to him, surely? Something which would bring him a good deal more hope, *and* a way forward. Until this moment, he had been stumbling through the shadows, unable to envision a single thing, whereas now he was able to stand in the light. Lady Charlotte had given him that.

I have so much to thank her for.

"And are you thinking of going this evening?" Lord Pottinger asked as Thomas slowly began to nod, only for Lord Wiltsham to interrupt

"Why do we need to wait until this evening? We have social occasions, certainly, but it is already late in the afternoon. We could go now. We could go at this very moment, in fact."

Lord Foster's eyebrows shot towards the ceiling and for a moment, it appeared as though he was about to protest, only for a broad grin to shoot across his face.

"A capital idea! We could take dinner at the club – you would have to accept my apologies, my dear lady – and thereafter, once we have attended this ball, we could return there again if required."

Lady Foster smiled indulgently at her husband, then looked towards Thomas.

"You may find that gentlemen are more willing to speak come the evening," she murmured. "Although I do think your suggestion a wise one. No time should be wasted. Shall I call for the carriage?"

In what appeared to be a flurry of relief and appreciation, Lord Foster practically jumped from his chair, hurried across the room, and took his wife's hands before pressing multiple kisses to the back of them. A little embarrassed at the scene, Thomas turned his head away, only for the other gentlemen to chuckle, although they were not laughing at him, nor his reaction, but rather at Lord Foster's enthusiastic admiration of his wife.

The jealousy which Thomas had pushed away once before began to curl itself upwards towards his heart, threatening to fill it, as Thomas caught the look of love which was shared between the couple. How much he longed for such a thing! He did not always feel it, but in moments like this, it became much too obvious. It was only when Lord Foster sat down again that the feeling began to fade, and he was able to smile again.

"My dear lady wife has released me and thus, we shall make our way to White's immediately." Lord Foster grinned, his eyes suddenly alive with both excitement and evident hope. "Are you ready, Silverton?"

Thomas nodded, suddenly slightly concerned that he might still be ignored should he walk into White's, only for his chin to lift and his resolve to strengthen.

"Yes, I am." Lord Foster slapped him on the shoulder and then turned towards the door, taking Thomas with him. With a deep breath, Thomas made his way outside towards the carriage, his hope building with every step he took. Just what was it that he would discover there?

~

WHITE'S WAS RATHER QUIET, but that was not surprising, given the hour. Walking inside, Thomas was hugely relieved when no one stopped him, although his heart immediately began to question why such a thing had not taken place. He expected that he would have been asked some rather important questions and asked whether or not he wished to settle his bill before taking his leave, but thus far neither thing had happened.

"You need not look so worried about your debt here. It has already been paid."

Thomas' eyes flared as Lord Stoneleigh grinned.

"I did not ask you to do that."

Lord Pottinger only laughed.

"We know you did not, and we were certain that, should you know of it or of our intentions beforehand, you would refuse to permit such a thing to take place. Therefore, it was done without your knowledge. Should you regain your fortune, you may repay it if you wish, but it is given to you with no obligation of repayment. Even if you should recover your fortune, none of us want this to be repaid. It is a gift, a recognition that you are in difficulty when we are not."

At this, Thomas smiled – albeit a little slowly – aware of the guilt which pierced his heart as he thought of his friends, not wanting any of them to consider that he was ungrateful. His reaction had been much too sharp.

"Thank you."

Mumbling a little, Thomas cleared his throat, trying to push away the awkwardness. Lord Stoneleigh chuckled, and Thomas' face burned, aware that he should have responded a good deal better than he had. It was his pride, he realized, pride which did not want the help of his friends. Pride that forced him to think he would have to face dark and difficult circumstances alone without even considering his friends. It did not sit well with him to accept charity from his friends, but then again, he supposed, it was the very sort of thing that he would have done himself, if he'd had the opportunity. A good deal more humbled, he sat down in a comfortable chair with his friends soon joining him.

"Mayhap some of us should move around the room a little," Lord Foster suggested astutely as Thomas nodded his agreement. "We shall speak to those who are present, note anyone else hidden in a corner, and thereafter, come back again and discuss what we have found... if anything."

"I quite agree. I shall stay here."

Thomas settled into his chair a little more and allowed his gaze to move around the room. There were not all that many gentlemen present. The only one he could see was one Lord Sotheby, who was currently asleep in his chair, his head dangling a little and his mouth ajar as he snored to himself. Thomas looked about the space again, spotting another chair in a quieter part of the room as his friends moved away, taking themselves to other areas of White's. Thomas frowned but remained where he was. Here, in a dark, secluded spot, he would be able to see those who came and went without making himself obvious to anyone.

Quietly ordering a brandy, he leaned back in his chair, accepting it without a word when it arrived. How long he sat he did not know, but the person at the forefront of his mind was none other than Lady Charlotte. He did not push thoughts of her away but allowed her to linger there. His interest in the lady had grown significantly, almost with every minute, now that he had allowed her to become a part of his life. At the same time, he realized how grateful he was for her, thankful that she had taken a risk in speaking with him so. How often had he pushed her away from his thoughts before now? How often had he refused to think about her, even though everything in him had wanted to do precisely that? A small smile graced his lips. He had no need to do such a thing now. He could think of her when-ever he chose, whenever he wished it, and for the moment, that was precisely what he wanted.

So deep were his thoughts, so many of them coming at once, that he almost did not notice when the door opened and closed again. Idly, he glanced towards the fellow who had come in, only to sit up straighter, his breath catching in his throat. The man wore his hat heavily over his eyes. His left hand was lifted to the brim, but his right hand remained down by his side, revealing his profile to Thomas. Blinking furiously, Thomas continued to stare at the man, watching as he sat down in a chair on the far side of the room. Still, Thomas could not keep his eyes from him, hardly able to believe what it was that he saw.

When the man removed his hat, Thomas closed his eyes, simply to calm himself down. It seemed as though Lord Foster had been correct after all, for there was no question about it now. The man sitting opposite Thomas, the man who had hidden himself away on the far side of the room, was none other than Lord Montague.

Uncertain as to how he ought to act, Thomas blinked rapidly, his mind turning over the many possibilities for what he could do, and what would happen thereafter. Should he remove himself from the room, then there was every chance that Lord Montague would see and recognize him, but should he remain here, then the chances of telling anyone else that Lord Montague was present were very slim indeed. His friends would not be anywhere near him at present.

Perhaps I should simply reveal myself to him.

Considering this, Thomas took a slow breath, trying, again, to consider what was best to do. His mind whirled around itself, and he simply could not think clearly, could not understand what was taking place. Why was Lord Montague present? Why was he back in England, and why would he *dare* to set foot in somewhere as public as White's?

As though Lord Montague himself knew that such a question was being asked, he rose suddenly as another gentleman approached. It was a man whom Thomas did not know. Lord Montague, on the other hand, appeared to be well acquainted with the fellow, for he greeted him quickly, but there was no smile as far as Thomas could see. They did not shake hands, and Lord Montague's frame was stiff as he inclined his head. All in all, it did not appear to be a very pleasant situation.

The two men sat down, with the second gesticulating furiously towards Lord Montague, who in response held up both hands in apparent defense of himself in the face of whatever this man was saying. It was not accepted, however, for the second man shook his head furiously and then slammed one hand down on the table. The sound echoed around the room, and Thomas immediately dropped his head, afraid that it would cause Lord Montague's eyes to scan around the room. When he dared another glance, however, the second man was leaning towards Lord Montague and clearly speaking in a furious whisper, and Lord Montague himself was shrinking back in his chair.

I do not recognize that gentleman, but maybe someone else will.

There was no other choice. He would have to go in search of one of his companions, for there was no wisdom in thinking to pursue Lord Montague on his own. Making his way as quickly as he could from his chair, Thomas hurried through the establishment in search of one of his friends. Finding Lord Wiltsham, he grasped the man's arm.

"Lord Montague is present. He is here."

Lord Wiltsham turned swiftly, his eyes wide, before he turned again on his heel and strode toward where Thomas had been. Catching him quickly, Thomas made his way directly back to his chair, leading Lord Wiltsham with him but, when he looked across the room, Lord Montague was nowhere to be seen.

"Where is he?"

Letting out a bellow of frustration which caught the attention of everyone else in the room and indeed, woke up Lord Sotheby, Thomas scowled angrily.

"He is gone."

A wry laugh burned through Lord Wiltsham's lips.

"Yes, I can see that. What was it he was doing? Why had he come here?"

Thomas threw up his hands, anger still burning through his veins.

"I do not know, other than that he was meeting with *that* gentleman. A fellow I did not recognize."

"The gentleman who is still sitting there?" Looking across the room, Lord Wiltsham gestured towards the gentleman whom Lord Montague had been speaking with, who was still sitting quietly, a drink in his hand. He was looking towards them both with interest, and Thomas immediately turned his face away.

"It may be that he knows who I am. He may tell Lord Montague that I was present here this evening."

"But *I* do not need to have any such fear."

Lifting his chin, Lord Wiltsham made to stride across the room, only for Thomas to catch his arm.

"Wait, what is it that you are doing?"

Lord Wiltsham shrugged.

"One of us must speak with him. You cannot do so, since there is a concern over the man's connection to Lord Montague. Therefore I shall. Do not fear, I will speak to you about it shortly."

Having no other choice but to sit down, Thomas did so reluctantly, glad that the shadows had kept his features a little hidden from the gentlemen across the room. A strain crept about his chest as he watched Lord Wiltsham approach the man, his hands clenching together. To his utter relief, the gentleman seemed glad to see him and indeed, Lord Wiltsham seemed to recognize the gentleman. Thomas managed a sip of his brandy, watching as the two men spoke for a few minutes. Thereafter, the gentleman gestured to the chair opposite and Lord Wiltsham immediately sat. Hearing the laughter echo across the room towards him, Thomas became more and more impatient with every minute that passed. His friend did not seem to be in any sort of hurry, for Lord Wiltsham and the gentleman spoke and laughed and drank as Thomas sat in the shadows, glowering over his now empty glass.

It was with some relief that Thomas watched Lord Wiltsham bid farewell to the gentleman, rising from his chair before shaking the man's hand. It was all he could do not to jump up from his chair and scurry toward Lord Wiltsham. Gripping the edge of the table, Thomas waited until his friend came to sit with him, remaining silent even as his friend grinned.

"Your patience is noted."

"I am not here for your compliments," Thomas shot back, managing a rueful smile. "Tell me, do you know that fellow?"

Lord Wiltsham nodded slowly, his grin beginning to fade away.

"Indeed I do. Only a little, you understand."

"But well enough to speak with him at length about the situation and what he knows of Lord Montague?"

"Of Lord Southend, you mean." Cocking one eyebrow, Lord Wiltsham sent a look in Thomas' direction. "That man does not know Lord Montague as Lord Montague. Instead, he knows him as Lord Southend."

Deeply confused, Thomas stared at him, but Lord Wiltsham only nodded, his gaze turning back to the gentleman opposite.

"You mean to say that he does not know Lord Montague by his true name?"

"Indeed, he does not," Lord Wiltsham answered, suddenly grave. "He is acquainted with him as Lord Southend, the gentleman with whom he played cards some months ago, and who has not repaid a significant debt. This afternoon's meeting was to clarify when the debt would be paid." His gaze slid towards Thomas. "Apparently this gentleman had been rather concerned as to Lord Southend's absence from London, quite certain that the fellow had run away with his funds. I am not certain of how he discovered Lord Montague again, but he made a great many threats. Finally those threats have been significant enough to have the man show his face here."

"Good gracious."

His breath seemed to fade out of him as Thomas ran his hand over his forehead, hardly able to believe what Lord Wiltsham had told him. Lord Wiltsham's dry chuckle had Thomas shaking his head in absent astonishment.

"It is most extraordinary," his friend agreed, "but it is to our advantage. We know now *one* of the reasons that Lord Montague is here in town. Clearly there have been some debts that he has been able to escape. If he is to regain his position in society – which is what I suspect he is eager to do, then he will have no other choice but to pay debts such as these."

"But if he has very little coin of his own, then how can such a thing be? Lord Foster took a great deal of it, did he not?"

"And therein lies the question." Lord Wiltsham smiled ruefully. "Lord Foster took back what was his, certainly, and he did not believe that Lord Montague was an overly wealthy fellow, for the man was much too inclined towards greed and liked to gamble as much as he could to gain as much as he could. I do not think that he was always success-ful, however!"

Thomas blew out a long breath.

"No, indeed."

"How long he has been in London, we do not know, but he *was* here, taking a meeting with another gentleman, in plain view of all who arrived. Most likely he considered this the safest place, given that he knows that the likes of you and I have not been frequenting this place."

Thomas nodded slowly.

"We shall have to tell Lord Foster."

"Indeed, we should. At once, in fact."

Taking a deep breath, Thomas let himself smile.

"It seems that this visit to White's was profitable after all, in a way that neither of us ever expected."

Lord Wiltsham nodded but did not smile.

"Let us hope that it leads us to something even greater," he replied. "We must pray that it will lead us to the truth as, for the moment, we have more questions than we do answers."

CHAPTER TWELVE

"I do hope that you have not been speaking with Lord Silverton."

Afraid that her eyes held a great deal of guilt, Charlotte immediately looked away from her mother.

"Why should you ask such a thing?"

Unwilling to lie, she dropped her gaze to her embroidery, which she had done very little of these last few months. Now it served as an excellent distraction from her mother's questioning looks.

Lady Landon's voice was a little harder.

"It is for good reason that I asked you to stay away from him, Charlotte. However, I have heard that you have been seen in his company quite recently. I can only hope that it was for some important reason which, I am afraid, you have yet to explain to me."

She dared a glance at her mother, and the urge to lie rose to her lips, but she quickly resisted it. The last thing she desired was to be dishonest, although she certainly would not tell her mother the entirety of the truth.

"I was speaking with him, yes." Aware of her mother's

rasping sigh, she tried to shrug. "It was a brief conversation, Mama, of no great seriousness. I am not often in his company and I am not caught up by him, if that is what you are concerned about."

Her heart twisted as she said these final words, aware that the desire in her heart was very much that she *was* caught by Lord Silverton. But as yet, nothing of substance had been spoken between them – a thought which was arrested as she then to recalled just how much there was of consequence going on at present.

"You are to stay away from him. I have made myself perfectly clear and I do not take kindly to your disobedience."

"You have, Mama, yes." Pressing her lips together for a moment, Charlotte took another breath. "As I have said, it was only a brief conversation, and you *did* state that brief conversations were permitted."

It was a little risky, perhaps, for her to speak so candidly, for her mother might then demand an even harsher situation between Charlotte and Lord Silverton, but she felt compelled to defend herself. Lady Landon opened her mouth, only to snap it closed, her eyes narrowing slightly as she regarded Charlotte, perhaps attempting to work out whether or not she spoke the entirety of the truth.

Charlotte looked back at her mother without guile. She had not said anything which was a lie, and her conscience was clear... thus far at least.

"I have not asked about him in some weeks, Mama." Continuing to speak quietly, Charlotte lifted one eyebrow. "I should be very grateful if you would tell me even a *little* about why I must stay away from him. My curiosity has not been sated, even though I have done what you ask."

A heavy sigh escaped from her mother's lips.

"You can be incorrigible, Charlotte."

A little humbled, Charlotte nodded her head in assent.

"Yes, Mama. I am aware of that."

She did not take back her question, however, allowing it to linger in the air between herself and her mother. Eventually, and with another formidable sigh, Lady Landon put out her hands, one to either side as she gazed at Charlotte steadily.

"The reason I did not say anything to you before now, Charlotte, was simply because I was afraid that you might have some... feelings... for Lord Silverton. In truth, I thought him an excellent gentleman. I was aware of your acquaintance and had every intention of encouraging you towards him."

Rather astonished, Charlotte lifted her gaze to her mother, her mouth a little ajar.

"I... I did not know."

"Precisely." Lady Landon smiled quietly. "My duty as your mother is to protect you and to guide you. That is what I have been doing – whether you are glad of it or not. I did not want to injure you by telling you the truth about Lord Silverton, for, if you had any sort of feelings for the gentleman, that might cause you further pain."

Charlotte licked her lips. She had a desire to discover the truth, but to do so would mean lying directly to her mother. Lord Silverton would be very glad indeed to find out why he had been so rejected, but she would have to pretend to her dear mother – who so clearly cared for her – that she had no feelings whatsoever for Lord Silverton, when quite the opposite was true. She had not told her mother the truth before, of course, but for whatever reason, to speak so now seemed to be a good deal more significant. It was as though in speaking words of denial, she would deny her heart. But what else was there for her to do? Her mother would not tell her the truth otherwise.

"You need have no concerns, Mama."

There now, she considered. That was not a lie, but neither was it the truth. For the moment, it would have to do.

"Very well." From the smile that followed, Charlotte assumed that it was something of a relief for her mother, now that she could be entirely truthful with Charlotte about Lord Silverton. "Then I shall tell you."

Charlotte sucked in a silent breath, waiting for her mother to speak, finding her heart beating so furiously that she was sure that the sound echoed around the room.

Sitting a little further forward in her chair, Lady Landon clasped her hands in her lap. Her gaze was fixed, and she looked at Charlotte steadily for some minutes without saying a single word, until Charlotte wanted to scream with frustration. In time, however, her mother's silent contemplations came to an end and with another heartfelt sigh, she shook her head.

"Lord Silverton does not want to marry. He has stated aloud that he will not betrothe himself this Season."

Charlotte stared at her mother, her heartbeat slowing as she attempted to make sense of what had just been said.

"Do you understand what I mean, Charlotte?" Lady Landon tilted her head a little, a gentle smile gracing her lips. "If he does not wish to marry, then I could not have you spending time with a gentleman who had no interest in securing a bride. I was aware that you were often seeking him out and I feared that such an eagerness would bring nothing but sorrow once you discovered the truth. Therefore, to protect you, I told you to stay far from him before any great feelings could develop."

Swallowing hard, Charlotte tried to find something to say, but the words would not come. Was this really what Lord Silverton had said? And if so, then who had he said it to? How had her mother come to know of such a thing? Question after question poured into her mind but she asked none of them. The consequences of this statement being true were severe indeed, for, if Lord Silverton truly had no wish to marry, then all of her feelings, all of the time that she had spent with him, the conversations she had enjoyed – it was all for nothing. Her mother did not know - could not know - of what she now felt, and for the present, Charlotte certainly could not inform her.

"You seem a little overwhelmed, my dear."

It was with evident concern that Lady Landon now looked at Charlotte, and Charlotte herself quickly forced a smile, having no desire to express to her mother what thoughts were currently in her mind.

"I am quite all right, Mama. It is only that I am surprised. He never gave such an impression to me."

"There was no call for him to." Lady Landon shrugged, rose, and made her way to the bell, clearly deciding that what Charlotte needed at present was a fortifying cup of tea. "Lord Silverton would have no need to express anything of that to you. You were merely an acquaintance, after all." Again, Charlotte said nothing, although that much, she had to silently admit, was true. She had only ever been an acquaintance to Lord Silverton. They had never meant anything of significance to each other. Even if she felt more, there was no promise that he felt the same. "Are you certain you are quite well?" Her mother pressed one hand to Charlotte's shoulder for a moment, before going to sit back down. "Your expression is very hard to make out at present, and I believe you have gone a little pale."

Before Charlotte could answer, a tap came at the door, signaling the arrival of the maid with the tea which Lady Landon had requested. Charlotte used the opportunity to pinch her cheeks, hoping that color would soon flood back into her face and relieve her mother's concern.

"I assure you that I am quite well." Forcing the brightest of smiles on her face, Charlotte sent it warmly across the room to her mother. "As I have said, I am a little surprised, that is all. Lord Silverton is considered an eligible gentleman by all of society, and he has never, to my knowledge, said anything to *any* young lady which might indicate that he has no intention of marrying. Might I ask, Mama, where you heard this from?"

Her mother allowed a small smile to lift the edge of her mouth, her eyes twinkling as though she were about to share some great secret.

"And I thought your curiosity was to be sated with this and this alone," she remarked as Charlotte blushed furiously.

"I am aware that I am full of questions, Mama, but I ask only because I am well aware of how little you are inclined towards gossip."

It was a good remark, for Lady Landon immediately nodded fervently, as though determined to express to her daughter that she was not in any way inclined towards rumors and the like.

"That is still very much the case. If you must know, it was an acquaintance of your father's who informed him of it."

At this Charlotte's astonishment blossomed into full bloom. Somebody had said such a thing to her father, which then meant, of course, that the news must have come from a gentleman rather than a lady. To her mind, that gave it a little more credence. Her heart sank very low indeed. Thankfully, any remark on her appearance was silenced by her mother serving the tea, and Charlotte was able to sit quietly and eat her cake without making any further remark on the subject of Lord Silverton and his lack of desire to wed. Much to her relief, her mother's conversation turned to other things, and she was left to consider the matter in her mind, making only the smallest of remarks here and there, whenever she felt able.

Her heart was distressingly heavy, however, her thoughts tumbling from one dark moment to the next. Lord Silverton had been the one to push her aside, had he not? He had been doing so out of chivalry, perhaps fully aware that he had no interest in marriage, perhaps concerned that she was considering him in a light that she ought not to be. Sipping the last of her tea, she thought about matters a little more. No, she concluded. Lord Silverton had told her about his fortune – or lack thereof – and had stated that *this* was why her mother had pushed her away from him.

Unless it is both his lack of fortune and *his lack of eagerness to wed.*

Setting her cup down, Charlotte set her shoulders. The best thing to do, she concluded, was to speak to Lord Silverton directly, to tell him that she had spoken with her mother, and provide him with a report of what her mother had said. She would tell him that, if such a thing were true, then she understood it. It would be a very difficult conversation indeed, but it was one that she would have to have regardless. Their acquaintance could continue, of course, but it would have to be nothing more than that. Nothing where she would allow her feelings to have any place. Perhaps, in time, they would fade, but for the present, they very much remained in the depths of her heart – and that now caused her a great deal of pain.

~

"You appear despondent."

Charlotte shook her head but did not look directly at her friend.

"I am not at all despondent."

The smile she forced was not believed, however, for Lady Florence immediately put one hand on her arm, her eyes going wide with evident concern as they stopped together, a light breeze catching Charlotte's curls.

"Something is wrong." Lady Florence did not turn her gaze away, reaching with her other hand to Charlotte's shoulder, as though she had very little intention of her letting her free until Charlotte told her the truth. Sighing, Charlotte tilted her head, but Lady Florence was unrelenting in her determination. "Pray tell me. I do not like to see you so."

"There is no need." Lady Florence ignored her, waiting in expectant silence. Seeing that there was no other choice but to tell her about Lord Silverton, Charlotte spread her hands. "My mother has informed me of why Lord Silverton is not to be in my company."

"Truly?" Releasing Charlotte's shoulder, Lady Florence stepped back. "And what is the reason? I am afraid it is significant given the expression on your face."

A sad smile creased Charlotte's features.

"Yes, yes, I suppose it is." Taking another breath, she looked away from her friend as she spoke. "Lord Silverton does not wish to marry. That is the reason my mother has given me for keeping me away from him. She was concerned that my feelings would become involved, and my heart would thereafter be broken when it became clear that he was not a gentleman even considering matrimony."

Lady Florence blinked rapidly. However, after some minutes she simply shook her head vehemently and, much to Charlotte's astonishment, laughed.

"You cannot be giving any credence to this idea, surely!"

Blinking in confusion. Charlotte paused for a moment before she responded, unsure as to what her friend meant.

"I am taking it with great seriousness."

"But why?" Lady Florence tipped her head. "You are as aware as I am that Lord Silverton is eager for your company. These last few days, his face has lit up the moment that you draw near. I have seen the change in his expression and I have seen how you have responded in turn! Do not think that there is anything of significance in that statement. Whether or not it is true, it will not be all that Lord Silverton feels. I am sure that you need not worry over what has been told to you."

At this, Charlotte found herself so astonished that she did not know what to say. Lady Florence laughed and comforted her a little more with words of a similar ilk, but Charlotte could still not take them in. Perhaps she *had* allowed fear to run through her a little too quickly. Perhaps she ought to have considered it all a little more carefully.

"Thank you, Florence." Taking in a breath, Charlotte was surprised at how quickly her frame seemed to loosen. "That has comforted me a great deal."

"I am glad." Lady Florence smiled, took Charlotte's arm, and they began to walk along together again. "Now, let us walk again before both our mothers call us and ask to know what it is that we are talking about, for I do not think I would be able to come up with any excuse!"

Charlotte laughed, a good deal happier already.

"Certainly."

Continuing to walk through Hyde Park, she allowed her mind to fill with thoughts of Lord Silverton – only for someone to catch her eye. Her swift intake of breath must have been heard by her friend, for Lady Florence swiveled her head sharply.

"What is it?"

Charlotte's eyes flared, her steps slowing as she saw watched none other than Lady Denfield take the arm of a gentleman and pull him a little away from the path, so that they were shaded from others in the park by a weeping willow.

"How very unusual."

"Is that... Lady Denfield?"

Charlotte nodded.

"It is." It was a little interesting to her that a lady of such distinction behaved in such a manner, particularly when they were in the middle of Hyde Park. "I do not think that I know that gentleman," she murmured, half to herself, half to Lady Florence. "Do you recognize him?"

"I did not get a good look at his face," Lady Florence replied quietly. "It is also unusual that they have attempted to hide themselves a little. Why would they do such a thing as that?" Frowning, Charlotte glanced over her shoulder. Their mothers were deep in conversation with each other and, having been walking a good deal more slowly than Charlotte and Florence, were a fair way behind them. So long as they were in sight, then all was well – which meant that they could slow their steps and even speak at length with Lady Denfield and her gentleman acquaintance, should they wish to. "What do you think we should do? If we walk past the weeping willow, we could simply ignore them."

Filling her lungs with air Charlotte decided to be bold.

"No. I think we should, at the very least, greet Lady Denfield. Who knows what we may discover?"

Before Lady Florence could protest, Charlotte immediately began to stride forward, only for her friend to take her hand and pull her back.

"What can you be thinking? It is clear that the lady is having a private conversation with that gentleman. It would not be right for us to interrupt."

Charlotte remained resolute.

"I believe we are quite within our rights to interrupt. In fact, I would almost say it is required of us." Continuing to walk forward, albeit a little more slowly, she pressed her friend's hand. "Recall that there is some concern as regards Lady Denfield. I do not think that standing here or, indeed, walking past them, would be wise. Lord Silverton must discover what it is that she is doing in keeping her close acquaintance with him and, even if this conversation with this particular gentleman leads to nothing other than mere introduction, at least we will have done something."

The more she spoke, the more her determination rose within her and it was a relief to see Lady Florence begin to nod slowly.

"Yes, I suppose that I can understand. It is more that it is a little unusual for ladies, such as ourselves, to interrupt such a conversation, however."

Charlotte smiled tightly, her eyes once more on the disguised figure of Lady Denfield, catching sight of her in between the branches of the weeping willow.

"Then let us make certain that we do not do so with any

plainness," she replied firmly. "Instead, let us be careful. Let us make it appear as though we are rather surprised to see her here. That way, she will think nothing of it."

Her breath quickened as she drew closer, Lady Florence beside her. Keeping her head forward, she looked out of the corner of her eye to see if she could see the lady a little better, and after a few moments, her cautiousness was rewarded. It was with a nudge to her friend that Charlotte turned her head, laughing brightly to make it appear as though she had found great mirth in something Lady Florence had said, only to exclaim with surprise.

"Lady Denfield? Good afternoon! I am not at all surprised that you have come for some shade under the tree, for it is very warm today, is it not?"

Smiling quickly, she immediately began to go towards the lady, ducking under a few tree branches. Lady Denfield swallowed hard as she turned towards Charlotte and Lady Florence, no smile of welcome on her face, although her voice was just as it usually was.

"Are you enjoying your afternoon walk, Lady Florence, Lady Charlotte? I confess it is *very* hot, yes."

Though she eventually managed to smile, Lady Denfield's gaze darted towards the gentleman at her side, just as Charlotte looked in his direction too. The gentleman did not appear to be at all at ease, for he quickly crossed his arms across his chest and turned his head away, one foot tapping impatiently on the ground as if to make it clear that she had interrupted something rather significant.

Charlotte stood quietly as Lady Florence stood beside her, her gaze still on the gentleman as they waited for the obviously required introduction. Lady Denfield's eyes went first to the gentleman, then back towards Charlotte and Lady Florence. She was obliged to introduce the fellow, and

Charlotte caught the slight flush which rose in the lady's face. What reason could there be for this?

"Forgive me, Lady Charlotte, Lady Florence. I have just been talking to an old acquaintance." Gesturing to the gentleman, Lady Denfield made a quick introduction. "This is Lord Southend. Lord Southend, this is Lady Charlotte and her friend, Lady Florence."

Charlotte blinked rapidly, rather taken aback at the quick and somewhat odd introduction. Lady Denfield had not told them the gentleman's title correctly, and nor had she given any indication that she was intending to do so. Given the silence which followed, it seemed as though the gentleman himself was to say nothing, for he made no attempt to show any sort of interest in the introductions. Rather, he merely turned his head towards them, nodded briefly, and then looked away again, without even a word of greeting.

"I am very pleased to make your acquaintance, Lord Southend." Charlotte clasped her hands in front of her, all the more surprised when the gentleman continued to remain silent. "I take it you are in London for the Season?"

"I am."

The man did not so much as glance at Charlotte but, instead, gave a long look towards Lady Denfield, before turning his head away again. It was as if he did not want to make himself at all recognizable to them, as if he was eager to hide his features as best he could. In doing such a thing, however, he was making himself all the more obvious to Charlotte.

"You must excuse me, but I must take my leave." Lady Denfield gave them both a quick smile, then immediately began to walk away. "I am certain that I shall see you on another occasion very soon"

Without so much as a murmur, Lord Southend followed her, but Charlotte's ears caught him muttering something towards Lady Denfield as they made their way past her.

"I told you that we should never have met out in the open. What a mess you have made of things now!"

Charlotte swung around, her eyes narrowing a little as she stared after the lady and the gentleman who were now departing from them as quickly as they could.

"What a rude fellow!"

Hearing the indignation in her friend's voice, Charlotte nodded her head slowly.

"Certainly, he was. I do not think that I have ever met a gentleman so impolite!"

"Really? A boorish gentleman? How very displeasing for you both – please, allow us to make up for his poor manner."

A familiar voice came to her ears, and Charlotte caught her breath. Suddenly hot, she hastily stepped out from under the weeping willow, seeing Lord Silverton standing with Lord Thornbridge, Lord Foster, and Lady Foster.

"It is good to see you." Speaking directly to Lord Silverton, even though there were others present, she flung one hand out a little behind her. "We have had a very strange meeting which has left us both rather confused indeed!"

Her eyes strayed over Lady Foster's shoulder to where her mother was following, but much to Charlotte's relief, she did not seem at all interested in who it was that Charlotte was talking with, choosing instead to talk to her friend.

Lord Silverton lifted his brows.

"Indeed. And who were you meeting with?"

"It was quite by accident," Lady Florence stated. "We saw Lady Denfield step under this tree with a gentleman.

After some minutes, we thought to introduce ourselves to him."

Charlotte's eyes returned to Lord Silverton, seeing a frown pull at his features.

"And this gentleman was one that you both found very ill-mannered?" Lord Foster asked as both Charlotte and Lady Florence nodded. "And why was that?

Charlotte rolled her eyes.

"He did not so much as *look* at us, did not ask me a single question, and Lady Denfield herself did not make the introductions properly."

"And that in itself was very odd, was it not?" Lady Florence asked as everyone nodded.

Lord Thornbridge chuckled.

"Most unusual. Who was he?"

Charlotte grimaced.

"Lady Denfield introduced him as Lord Southend, although I do not know whether he is a Viscount, an Earl, a Marquess, or even a Baron!"

It was as though lightning had struck them all. The smiles shattered on every face and the breath which was taken in was an obvious one, as all of the gentlemen pulled air sharply into their lungs at the same time. Every person stared at her for some moments in complete silence. Charlotte could not understand why they were silent and looked from one to the other. Was something wrong with what she had said?

"Lord Southend?" Lord Silverton spoke quickly, taking a half step closer and putting his hand on her arm. "You are certain that she said Lord Southend?"

"Yes, of course I am certain. She departed with him only a few moments ago, in fact."

"Where?" Lord Silverton's voice had risen, the tightness

of his fingers on her arm growing steadily. "Where did this gentleman go, Lady Charlotte? In what direction?"

She pointed, wordlessly, and to her utter astonishment, the gentlemen took to their heels at once, hurrying past them, running through Hyde Park, and hurrying in the direction that she had given Lord Silverton. Only Lady Foster remained with Charlotte and Lady Florence.

"I am left to explain to you it seems," Lady Foster remarked, softly. "But what I *will* say at present is that it may be that you have managed to bring this dire situation to an end, Lady Charlotte. And if that is so, then we shall all be very grateful to you indeed."

CHAPTER THIRTEEN

*G*reat heaving breaths tore from Thomas' lips. He was all too aware of the scene he was making, running with such haste through Hyde Park at what was now almost the fashionable hour, but he did not care. Lord Foster and Lord Wiltsham ran with him, each on the heels of the other as they rushed in the direction which Lady Charlotte had pointed them in.

We have to find him. He cannot be that far.

Pain tore through his chest as his lungs began to burn and sparks came into his vision. His steps slowed until he could not take another step. Putting his hands on his thighs, he bent forward, gasping for breath as his friends came to stand beside him – both in the same position as him.

"We have lost him."

Lord Pottinger's harsh tones reached Thomas' ears as he lifted his head, seeing the many other people in Hyde Park watching them. A few laughed and some clapped, clearly thinking that they had taken on a race against each other, so that they might impress a lady. Rising all the more, he lifted a hand to wave at those who watched, frustration building with every single breath he took. How was it that he could have lost Lord Montague when he had only been a few minutes ahead of them?

"Good gracious, that was rather impressive!" A gentleman Thomas vaguely recognized strolled over, slapping one hand on Thomas' back. "I should say that you won there, old boy, although quite why *you* are trying to impress a particular young lady I cannot imagine."

Such was Thomas' irritation that he pushed out a response before he could prevent it.

"The financial standing of myself and any possible future wife is entirely my own concern, *not* the concern of the *ton*."

The gentleman blinked and rubbed one hand over his chin.

"Financial standing?" he asked, as Thomas slowly straightened, his chest still heaving furiously. "I do not know anything about that, I confess! I was simply remarking upon the fact that it would be strange for a gentleman who has sworn not to marry this Season to now be doing all he can to impress a young lady!"

"I beg your pardon?"

Becoming all the more confused by every word the gentleman said, Thomas looked at his friends in turn but they all either shrugged or shook their heads, clearly as confused as he.

"You have not taken back your bet, have you?" the man asked, suddenly sounding rather urgent as Thomas' frown grew heavier still. "I have a great deal of money on Lord Southend winning against you, I confess! Perhaps foolishness, but I was convinced by his confidence."

Whatever is he speaking of?

Lord Foster came towards them, to stand beside the

fellow in question, a smile on his face which made him appear quite amiable.

"You are speaking of the bet in White's betting book, are you not?"

The gentleman's face immediately split into a grin, clearly relieved that someone knew what he was talking about.

"Yes, that is it precisely. I shall not say more, for fear that I have already overstepped, but if you have joined the bet, Lord Foster, then I wish you every success, regardless of which side you are on!"

Lord Foster nodded, smiled tightly, and much to Thomas' relief, then stepped away. Thomas immediately swung his gaze towards his friend, but Lord Foster held up both hands, palms towards him.

"Before you ask, no, I did not know any of this. It was a guess only."

Instantly, Thomas' defenses dropped.

"A guess?"

Lord Foster nodded.

"Recall that Lady Charlotte overheard talk of the plotters' desire to keep you away from White's – has not that reason now become clear? There is a bet in the betting book that you must not be permitted to see... that would be my assumption, anyway, given what that rather outspoken gentleman has admitted to us."

"I am glad that he did so." Thomas admitted this with a brief smile, and took in a huge breath, his heart slowly returning to a regular rhythm. "I am only sorry that we did not catch Lord Montague – or Lord Southend, as he is apparently known to some."

"Only to those who do not know him as Lord Montague," Lord Pottinger put in, a grim smile on his face.

"I am quite sure that he is being very careful indeed about who he speaks with."

"With one of those being Lady Denfield," Lord Wiltsham remarked, as he too finally came into a standing position rather than being hunched forward. "There is something significant in that. You have a great deal to thank Lady Charlotte for, Silverton. I do not think that any of us would have known of this if she had not been bold enough to tell you what she had overheard." Thomas nodded slowly, thinking to himself that there was more than just appreciation in his heart when it came to Lady Charlotte. "What then shall we do?" Lord Wiltsham asked, looking around Hyde Park as though he might somehow find a glimpse of Lord Montague. "How are we to catch both Lady Denfield *and* Lord Montague and, in doing so, make sense of all of this?"

"I do not think that we need to catch them both." Considering for a moment, Thomas tilted his head to one side as he thought out loud. "Lady Denfield is the one we must speak with first. She has a good deal more to lose than Lord Montague. Lord Montague seems to care for nothing but coin, and for no one save for himself, but Lady Denfield has very little else in this world, except for her reputation." Wincing, he shrugged his shoulders. "I should not like to do it, but if I must, we will have to threaten her to find out what exactly she has been doing with Lord Montague and how such a partnership came to be."

"I think your heart is still inclined to believe that she is an unwilling participant in all of this."

Turning his head upon hearing the new voice enter their conversation, Thomas' heart skipped at the sight of Lady Charlotte, her hand reaching out to take his, even though they were in the middle of Hyde Park. He took it quickly, drawing her close to his side as Lady Foster and Lady Florence came to join them. He guessed that they had all been walking quickly across the park, given the fact that Lady Charlotte's breathing was coming a little faster than usual and there was a pink flush in the depths of her cheeks.

"What do you mean, Lady Charlotte?"

Lady Charlotte held his gaze steadily.

"Lady Foster has explained what she can, as regards your fortune, Lord Montague, and all that has taken place. I believe that you are much more inclined to think that Lord Montague is the one to blame and that he has perhaps dragged Lady Denfield into this situation without her full willingness. But given what I heard in the bookshop, given the delight in her voice as she spoke, I am leaning towards the thought that she is as much involved in this as Lord Montague has been. Perhaps there is some connection between them, which as yet we do not know of."

Thomas could not help but press her hand, grateful, once again, for her insight and her willingness to speak openly. There was no question in his mind about Lady Charlotte, for his desire to become closer to her still grew steadily – but that could not be until this mystery came to its conclusion... which made him all the more eager for such a thing to be so.

"You are right, Lady Charlotte," he admitted quickly. "There are some things I still need to consider a good deal more carefully." Catching a slightly concerned glance from Lord Foster, he repositioned himself so that his hand which clasped Lady Charlotte's would be hidden from the prying eyes of those around them "I should also tell you that there has been a bet placed about me in White's betting book. We found this out unexpectedly, and I confess that I am rather surprised to hear it. As yet, I do not know what it is but –"

"I believe I might!" Lady Charlotte's eyes had suddenly gone very wide indeed and, as Thomas looked down at her, he saw them widen further still. "In fact, I think I understand it all."

"What is it?" Lord Foster asked, sounding almost as eager as Thomas felt. "What is it that you understand, Lady Charlotte?"

Lady Charlotte took a breath.

"My mother has long told me to stay far from Lord Silverton," she said softly. "I have told you that myself, have I not?"

Her eyes went back to his and Thomas nodded quickly.

"Yes, indeed you have. That is true."

Lady Charlotte held his gaze for a moment.

"You stated that it was because of your fortune, because you believed that society knew of how little wealth you had. Is that not so?"

Slowly, Thomas nodded, lines forming across his forehead as he frowned.

"But that is not the reason behind it, not at all."

Thomas blinked, surprise forming a ball in his chest.

"It is not?"

Both Lady Charlotte and Lady Florence shook their heads.

"My mother has only just informed me that I am to stay far from Lord Silverton because, as she stated, 'he has no desire to marry'." One shoulder lifted. "You have no intention to betrothe yourself to any young lady this Season, apparently."

"And my mother states the same."

It was Lady Florence who spoke as Lady Charlotte nodded. The ball in Thomas' chest suddenly exploded as he slowly began to understand. Air seemed to freeze in his lungs, the noise of the people around him fading as he looked back into Lady Charlotte's face. Everything had been so very confusing, but slowly, it was beginning to become clear.

"All this time, I have believed that the reason that not only you but the other young ladies in London were being kept back from me was that society knew of my loss of fortune. Now you tell me that it is because they believe I do not want to wed?"

Lady Charlotte gave him a small smile.

"Yes. This is not about your fortune."

"We have all been mistaken," Lady Foster murmured. "Does society know at all about your fortune, then?"

"I should think it does not." Finally, Lady Charlotte pulled her gaze away from Thomas, looking towards Lady Foster instead. "My mother made no mention of such a thing. In fact, I would be very surprised indeed if very many people at all knew of it. For whatever reason, everyone in society believes that you have declared that you will not marry this Season. That I believe, is what this will be about."

Thomas scrubbed one hand over his face. This was almost too extraordinary to take in! When had such a bet taken place – and why? He could not remember saying anything of the sort.

Wait a moment.

A sudden memory came back to him as he recalled the night he had been drinking heavily at White's, remembering how he could not recall a single thing that had happened once Lord Thornbridge had left. Closing his eyes, a quiet groan escaped his lips.

Immediately, Lady Charlotte's hand tightened on his.

"My Lord...?"

"I am not distressed." He answered her quickly, hearing the concern in her voice. "Rather, I am ashamed. I do not know for certain, but I believe that on the night I discovered my fortune was gone, I may have said something along those lines. I was in a very dark frame, believing that my entire fortune was gone from me, believing that I would never marry, could never offer my hand to some young woman, for my lack of fortune would bring her no happiness or content-ment. It would not surprise me, therefore, if I said such a thing and, in the days thereafter, someone then placed a bet upon me, stating either that they would be able to force my hand in one way or another, or would be able to find someone to turn my head."

Lord Foster cleared his throat.

"We did, in fact, see Lord Montague at White's only recently, did we not? Given that he has chosen to return to England for some reason – but again, without the fortune which he had stolen from Lord Foster – what if he heard about your declaration, saw an opportunity, and thereafter decided to place a bet, having a scheme in mind to make certain of his success?"

"It is all hypothetical thus far." Lord Wiltsham frowned as Thomas himself considered the suggestion. "But there is a way that we will be able to find out the truth." Setting his shoulders, he clapped Thomas on the back. "I will go to White's. I will find the betting book, and I will look inside. I do not think that it would be wise for *you* to do so, for fear that Lord Montague may be watching and will see that you have become aware of the situation."

Thomas gritted his teeth, seeing the wisdom in Lord Wiltsham's suggestion, but at the same time finding himself very eager indeed to be the one to find out what was written there about him. It was only Lady Charlotte's squeeze of his hand which encouraged him to take a breath as he acknowledged that Lord Wiltsham's thoughts held the path that ought to be taken.

"Very well."

"We must continue as normal. There is to be a ball this evening, and I expect that Lady Denfield will be present." Taking a breath, he looked around at the group of his friends, feeling himself so close to the end of what had been a very difficult trial for him. "We shall have to speak to Lady Denfield directly and tell her that we know the truth. If you, Wiltsham, have discovered what we think is there within the White's betting book, then when such a conversation happens, Lord Foster should be present also, to hear all from her. I am certain that she will have no other choice but to confess the truth – and in doing so we will be able to capture Lord Montague."

"And thereafter regain your fortune," Lord Wiltsham said quietly. "Lord Montague is a man filled with such greed that I do not think I have ever seen the like before. He seems to be willing to do anything he can to gain whatever he can. What he has is never enough for him. We shall have to find a way to force his hand, but that will come later. Let us, for the moment, think only of Lady Denfield and how to gain the truth from her. Perhaps from there, we will find a way forward."

Lady Charlotte looked up at Thomas.

"I should like to be there," she said quietly, her eyes flickering with concern. "I should like to hear Lady Denfield make her explanations for what she has done. I would like to stand alongside you and let her see that her attempts to encourage you toward a close relationship with her have failed."

Thomas let his fingers thread through hers, heedless of

those who stood near them, those who might watch them at the present moment.

"I can assure you, my dear lady Charlotte, that her efforts have *indeed* failed," he said softly. "I have never felt anything for the lady, not even a single flicker of emotion. There was a time when I was grateful for her friendship, fearful that society was about to turn its back on me, but since then, I have found myself coming to understand that there is a greater joy in one singular connection than there could ever be through a whole host of others."

When the color lifted in Lady Charlotte's cheeks and her eyes began to dazzle with light, Thomas simply smiled at her, wishing that he could pull her into his arms. She understood, then, that he was talking only of her, telling her, as best he could, that his connection with her was the most important one to him. Once this matter was at an end, he prayed that he would be able to consider it all the more deeply.

"Until this evening, then." Lady Foster's voice was soft, but it broke Thomas' connection with Lady Charlotte. "Let us pray that this is the end of the matter, once and for all."

CHAPTER FOURTEEN

"*A*h, there you are, Lord Silverton."

The merry voice of Lady Denfield reached Thomas' ears as he turned to face her, immediately covering Lady Charlotte's presence by standing directly in front of her – just as they had expected he might have to do. Near him, there also lingered Lord Wiltsham, Lord Pottinger, Lord Stoneleigh, Lord Thornbridge, and Lord and Lady Foster. But as yet, Lady Denfield did not seem to even notice them, given the way that her eyes caught – and held – to his. His stomach twisted as he demanded his lips curve into a smile that he did not really feel. The truth was that, at the present moment, he despised everything that Lady Denfield offered him. Her smiles were nothing, her laughter false, and the light in her eyes was only a pretense. He had discovered the truth.

Lord Foster *had* found Thomas' name in the betting book – albeit a couple of pages back – and the bet itself had been placed there by one Lord Southend, who had stated that Thomas would find himself betrothed by the very end of the Season. A few discreet enquiries had led

164 | ROSE PEARSON

to the discovery that Thomas' assumption had been correct – he *had* made a declaration that night, of his intent not to marry, in the time after Lord Thornbridge had left.

And Lord Montague, in his guise as Southend, had seen his opportunity.

Given that Thomas himself had declared that he would not become betrothed during the summer Season, the likelihood of such a thing occurring had been very slim indeed, and thus a great many bets had been placed upon Lord 'Southend's' proposal. Thomas was now quite certain that Lady Denfield was meant to be the person he betrothed himself to. The fact that she was working with Lord Montague made something hard kick in his stomach as he put on a smile, hating that he had to pretend so. The only thing in his heart for Lady Denfield was disdain.

"Good evening, Lady Denfield!" Keeping his voice warm, he inclined his head. "The ball is already underway. I do hope that you are to dance this evening?"

Thomas' skin prickled at the thought of dancing with her, but all the same, he accepted her dance card, putting his name to one of the dances near the end of the evening, knowing that he would be saved from actually standing up with her. With a smile, he handed the card back to her, relieved to know that his friends were nearby, watching everything which took place. Somehow, he would have to find a way to lead Lady Denfield towards a quieter part of the ballroom, where he might be able to speak with her directly.

"I am very grateful," Lady Denfield's fingers brushed his as she accepted it, although Thomas had to resist the urge to pull his hand back sharply. "I wonder if you are not particularly busy if you would like to take a short walk with me? The room is rather stuffy, and I find myself looking for a little fresh air."

Thomas' eyebrows lifted in surprise, but he covered this quickly by inclining his head.

"Yes, of course. I quite understand how you feel. The doors are open at the end of the ballroom. However, we could go and stand near them if you should like."

"Mayhap we could step outside?"

Nodding, Thomas offered his arm.

"If you are feeling a little warm, then I should not want you to become overwhelmed."

"You are a most gracious gentleman, Lord Silverton." Lady Denfield continued to smile up at him as they made their way slowly to the other side of the ballroom. "I confess that I do not think I have ever met another gentleman such as you, in all of my time in London."

Not at all touched by her flattery, Thomas murmured his thanks but kept his gaze straight ahead, choosing not to look at her for fear that she would see the truth in his eyes.

"That is very kind of you to say."

"I mean every word."

Remembering that he was meant to be giving the appearance of embracing their connection, Thomas shook his head.

"I think your compliments are a little too fine, my dear lady," he remarked, giving her a wry smile so that she would not think him harsh, but rather protesting lightly at her words. "I have many faults, I can assure you."

Lady Denfield laughed.

"*You*, Lord Silverton, are a gentleman who is unused to taking compliments from a lady such as me," she stated. "But I shall forgive you for that, given our close acquaintance."

Approaching the open French doors, Thomas gestured towards them with his free hand.

"You wish to step outside still?"

Her nod was her assent and Thomas led her out at once, giving only a quick glance over his shoulder to assure himself that his friends were following him.

The gardens were fairly large, and all around were torches that lit the night darkness with a great many flames. Thomas walked silently alongside Lady Denfield, making their way towards a quieter part of the gardens where the shadows grew thicker, although he could still see her face.

Their steps slowed and, much to Thomas' surprise, Lady Denfield swung around to face him, her chin tilted as though she were incredibly eager to press her lips to his – and Thomas immediately stepped back.

"Lord Silverton?"

Thomas lifted his chin.

"Lady Denfield. Where is Lord Southend – or, should I say, Lord Montague?"

Seconds of silence ticked by, and Lady Denfield only stared back at him, her face pale in the dim light. As he continued to wait, her hands slowly reached toward her face, pressing hard against her lips as she gave a small shake of her head.

"You need not pretend any longer, Lady Denfield." It was Lady Foster who spoke, her voice emerging from the darkness. Someone stepped beside him, brushing against his shoulder. Thomas did not even need to look to know that was Lady Charlotte. "We know that you are in league with Lord Montague, Lady Denfield." Lady Foster continued to speak, her voice calm but firm. "Although why you are willing to involve yourself in such an evil as this is quite beyond me."

Lady Denfield closed her eyes and again, shook her head.

"I do not know what you mean."

Her voice wobbled with evident emotion, but Thomas' lip curled at the sound. He did not believe it for a moment.

"You have just heard me say that we know it all." Lord Wiltsham took a small step closer to the lady, and each of Thomas' other friends came to stand with him, forming a semi-circle around Lady Denfield. "I went to White's and discovered the bet and Lord Montague's name. Given that Lord Silverton had stated – in a somewhat drunken manner, I believe – that he would not marry this Season, the bet seems an excellent one for the reward would be significant, should Lord Silverton find himself betrothed. Lord Montague is seeking to gain as much wealth for himself as possible – and, therefore, the reason for your acquaintance with Lord Silverton has become quite clear."

"And it is thanks to Lady Charlotte's careful consideration and willingness to tell me all that I find that I am not taken in."

Unable to help himself, he slipped an arm around her waist, and immediately, Lady Charlotte moved closer.

"I... I..."

It appeared as though Lady Denfield could not find a single word to say in response to all that they had set before her. Her eyes were darting from one side to the other, her hands opening out wide, only to drop back to her sides.

"You will tell us why you have been working for Lord Montague," Lord Pottinger murmured quietly. "Again, do not protest that you have no knowledge of him. We are well aware that *you* are the one who is meant to betrothe yourself to Lord Silverton, one way or the other. That way Lord Montague will win his bet and become a very wealthy man indeed, and no doubt he will give you a decent share of his profits."

"I had no other choice," Lady Denfield's desperate words came out in a whine. "There was nothing I could do, nothing that I could say that would prevent him from taking advantage of me, from forcing my hand!" Clasping her hands together at her heart, she turned her attention to Thomas, her eyes glistening with evident tears. "I swear to you that I had no other choice but to do as was asked. Lord Montague demanded that I obey him, and if I did not, then there would have been terrible consequences."

"It is astonishing to me that you can lie so brazenly."

Before Thomas could respond, Lady Charlotte spoke up, releasing herself from Thomas' hand.

"We have told you already that there is only one thing required of you. We want you to tell us the truth, and yet you persist in attempting to undermine us. Do you not understand, truly? You were overheard that day in the book-shop, and I myself was witness to the fact that you found great joy in the situation in which you placed Lord Silverton. You may think that you will be able to pretend, Lady Denfield, to twist your way out of this, but I assure you that you cannot. You were delighted to think of betraying Lord Silverton's trust. To my mind, I believe that you were eager to look up at him and to declare your love, only to leave him at the altar on the very day of your marriage." Her voice rose suddenly, her words forceful. "In fact, I have every belief that you would then have taken great pleasure in telling the *ton* all about Lord Silverton's lack of fortune so that you might save your own reputation and have society feel sorry for you. They would declare you innocent and decry Lord Silverton. That was what you wanted, was it not? That was your intention. For whatever reason, you and Lord

Montague have every intention of making as much of a mockery of Lord Silverton as you can."

"It was not just of him."

The explosion that tore from Lady Denfield's lips was enough to send Thomas' heart into a flurry. In losing her decorum, she had declared her guilt. There could be no turning back from this now.

"What do you mean?" Speaking firmly, Thomas caught Lord Foster's presence beside him. "You mean that you have been involved in all of this. From the very beginning, you have assisted Lord Montague in his dark plans. You helped him as he arranged for many a gentleman to be taken to the East End, whereby they would then go on to lose their fortune. The six of us were unfortunate enough to be caught up in such a scheme, but I am certain that there were others before us. Is that not so?"

The only sound which came in answer to his question was the noise of the ball from behind him. The music and the laughter were anathema, his stomach tightening as everyone looked toward Lady Denfield. She had dropped her head into her hands and, this time, Thomas was not certain that she was acting in that manner to garner sympathy – sympathy which, regardless, he was not about to give.

"It is all true." Lady Charlotte spoke softly, and Lady Denfield did not protest. "But why? Why would you help someone such as Lord Montague? I do not understand."

"Because he is my brother." Lady Denfield lifted her head, her hands clenching into fists as she held them taut by her sides. "When Lord Foster thought to send him to the continent, I had other ideas. I took the money I had left to me from my late husband, and gave all of it to him, to make certain that he could return to England. Every single penny was offered, and it was taken, but it brought my brother back so I considered it worthwhile. But my brother was determined that I should be given recompense. It was only by chance that he heard about your declaration, Lord Silverton." She lifted her chin, her eyes flashing. "When you returned to London, my brother saw his chance, and the scheme was prepared. It was easy enough, and you seemed very eager indeed for company. Lord Montague believed that you would not come to White's again, given that you had declared such a thing that very same night, and because he knew of your lack of fortune." The harsh laugh which followed made Thomas wince – only for something to snap into sharp clarity in his mind.

"Wait a moment." Stepping forward, he grasped Lady Denfield's arm hard, his chest suddenly tight. "Lord Montague knew I had lost my fortune. He knew then who had stolen it from me that night."

Lady Denfield laughed scornfully.

"*I* did," she stated plainly, as Thomas dropped her arm in sheer astonishment. "You may not recall, but you attempted to leave the gambling den. For some minutes, I was afraid that I had lost you – only to discover you in the care of two ragamuffins who I very easily used for my own purposes. I accompanied you to your townhouse, begged for your staff to permit me to make certain that you were well – and in my time in your house, forged a letter, using your own seal, to tell your solicitors that they were to move your fortune to another account with all swiftness." She shrugged lightly, a delighted smile on her lips. "They were remarkably fast, and my brother moved the money again the very moment that it arrived."

Thomas closed his eyes, his throat constricting. It seemed as though Lady Denfield had decided to tell them all, holding nothing back, and perhaps now realizing that she had no excuses left to give.

"Then Lord Montague tricked not only Lord Foster, but myself."

"And he was successful, was he not?"

The pride in Lady Denfield's voice made a flood of anger suddenly burn in Thomas' chest and he found himself going even closer to her, looming over her, hating her smile.

"Your brother has no sense of loyalty. You gave all that your late husband's family left to you to facilitate his return to England. He ought to have repaid that from his own fortune, ought to have given you *more* to offer you a secure future. Instead, he chose to cheat it out of someone else."

Lady Denfield did not so much as flinch, confidence flooding into her voice.

"I do not care how my brother gains the wealth he wishes to give me. And truth be told, I rather like the idea of being as wealthy as Croesus. You think that I have no conscience?" Her cold laugh ran around Thomas' frame, making him shudder. "Mayhap that is so, but if I am the same as my brother, then I am proud of that fact."

It was as though she were someone entirely different standing before him; a lady whom Thomas did not know, and certainly did not recognize. She had transformed into her true appearance now, for this was Lady Denfield as she truly was. His whole body shivered, his stomach dropping as he looked into her face and saw the ice and steel which was settled in her gaze. How fortunate he had been to escape from her.

"Where is your brother?"

Lady Denfield shook her head and laughed again.

"Do you think that I will tell you?"

Lady Foster stepped forward, moving towards Lady Denfield with swift steps. Her voice was low, but it was firm.

"Understand this, Lady Denfield. You may hide your brother's presence from us, but I can assure you that we will find him nonetheless."

"And just how do you intend to do that?" Lady Denfield sneered. "There is nothing that you can do or say which will force my hand."

"That is true. Therefore, we shall simply be in your company until your brother decides to call upon you again," Lady Foster replied firmly. "Do not think that you will be able to warn him. You will not be able to do a thing to tell him that we are waiting. He has caused a severe injury to all of us present here – and you shall not be free of our company until we find Lord Montague again."

The tension which then swept between the group was like a strong wind that buffeted them all about. Instinctively, Thomas stepped back to Lady Charlotte, reaching out one hand to her as though he wanted to protect her, but while she took his hand, there was a gentle smile on her face which chased away his concern. He knew now that, regardless of what happened, his friends would make certain that he was no longer stuck in difficulty – but more than that, he would have Lady Charlotte with him; a lady who had refused to step aside, had refused to ignore the concern she had felt for him, who had seen the difficulties and had not run from them. He was grateful for her, more grateful than he thought he could ever express. Perhaps the only way would be to ask her to be by his side for his future, so that he might spend every day attempting to do so. He had everything he would ever need in Lady Charlotte. He had comfort, he had hope, he had trust, he had joy, and that,

Thomas understood, was a good deal more comforting and desirable than any financial satisfaction and comfort could ever be.

Lady Denfield's harsh snort broke into his thoughts.

"You cannot do such a thing."

This time, it was Lord Foster who spoke, laughing softly as he came close to his wife, and Thomas found himself smiling, his hope bolstered.

"I think you will find that we can," Lord Foster returned. "Come now. Lady Denfield, depart from this place if you wish, but have every assurance that we will be with you. We will be watching you. We will be in the same room as you, even if you are at home. You may try to turn us from your house if you wish, but I have every confidence that a Marquess will not be refused entry." Turning, he gestured to Lord Stoneleigh. "Perhaps it is that we should have to involve the King. You do know that Lord Stoneleigh is well acquainted with the King, do you not?"

Lord Stoneleigh chuckled.

"I am indeed."

Lady Denfield's gasp was so evident to all of them that Thomas found himself smiling broadly, aware that the lady's confidence was eroding. They would find Lord Montague within a day, he was sure. Whether she wished it or not, Lady Denfield's brother would be discovered and one way or another, Thomas would regain his fortune.

"He has taken rooms on Straight Street." Lady Denfield's voice was low, her head hanging forward as though she were utterly dejected, forced into giving information she had no desire to give up. "You will find him there this evening."

Thomas' mouth fell open, but Lady Charlotte squeezed his hand quickly, her eyes filled with a sudden and furious fire. He could hardly believe it – but it seemed as though Lady Denfield's confidence was just as brittle as her brother's thoughtfulness. Both fell apart much too easily.

"I think it is best that Lady Foster and Lady Charlotte remain here."

Lord Foster spoke quickly, as Thomas pulled himself from his astonishment.

"Stoneleigh, might you linger also? The rest of us will make our way directly to Straight Street."

As Lord Stoneleigh nodded his assent, Thomas turned quickly to Lady Charlotte.

"My dear lady." Grasping both her hands, he pressed them earnestly. "Rest assured that I will call upon you tomorrow, at my earliest convenience. I am sure I will have much to tell you."

She looked into his eyes for a long moment.

"Of course, Lord Silverton. I look forward to seeing you tomorrow, and wish you every success." Bending her head, she kissed his fingers, then smiled gently. "Come back to me soon."

≈

"And so you are not on the continent, as we thought."

Thomas watched as Lord Montague attempted to get out of his chair before falling back. His eyes were fixed on Lord Foster, a garbled sound coming from his throat. One hand gripped the arm of his chair, the other waving out in front of him frantically, as though he could somehow disperse away the vision of the gentlemen coming into his rooms.

"You did not think that you would be discovered, did you?" Thomas shook his head. "You became too confident, much too sure of your own abilities. I assume, no doubt, that you were originally to be hiding away, but as time went on, you grew bolder, telling only those who did not know you of your supposed title of 'Southend'. You decided you could not remain in hiding for so long, not when there was money to be gained! Did you find a few more people to fleece? Some more poor fellows to try to steal from?" Lord Montague closed his eyes, one hand going to his throat, his face puce. "You heard of my foolish talk, did you not? Even though you were not present your-self at the time, you chose to make a bet and used your sister to attempt to succeed." The fact that silence came from Lord Montague convinced Thomas that every word was true. "Your sister deserves the punishment as much as you," he stated firmly. "But the fact that you used her in your schemes makes you a good deal more culpable... even if she states that she very much enjoyed taking what belongs to others for herself."

Lord Montague closed his eyes, leaning his head back against his chair as though he might faint from the shock of being discovered. Thomas was quite certain that it came from an arrogance, a belief that he was much too clever to be found out. That pride had led to little slips here and there until, at last, the truth was finally out.

"My sister has nothing to live on," Lord Montague protested, his voice thin. "After her husband died, she was left with very little. Her late husband's family would not give her what they ought to have done."

"Then they are just as cruel, as greedy, and selfish as you." Lord Wiltsham remarked dryly. "But you need not lie. Your sister told us that she gave all her money to bring you back from that ship bound for the continent – but rather than repay her with your own coin, albeit coin stolen from others, you chose to come up with yet another scheme by which you might make certain of her future security."

"Your selfishness is astounding." Anger began to burn in his heart, sending fire through Thomas' veins. "You did not even want to give your own sister a single penny. Therefore, you determined that you would find a way to gain wealth in another manner to pass it to your sister. There is never enough money for you to be satisfied. You always wish to acquire a little bit more, never willingly giving a single coin away."

Lord Montague did not say a single word. This was not the brave charlatan Thomas had once known! Instead, Montague seemed to shrink into this chair, finally defeated.

Thomas lifted his chin, glanced at Lord Foster, and nodded.

"You have a choice." Lord Foster's voice was low and dark. "You can show a *single* bit of consideration towards your sister, or you can continue to be as selfish as you have always been. This is your chance to finally show some brotherly affection."

Lord Montague looked up, wide-eyed, staring into Lord Foster's face.

"I... I do not understand what you mean."

"You are to return to the continent, of course." Lord Foster now spoke quite calmly, as though Lord Montague should have expected such a thing. "You will not return from there for many years, realizing, I hope, that you will no longer be well-liked here in England. Have no doubt, Lord Montague, everything you have done will be told to all of society – and, in fact, to the King, courtesy of Lord Stoneleigh. For now that all of us have– or will soon have – regained our fortunes, there can be no shame in stating everything which has taken place. Whenever you decide to return, you will not be given a single glance of welcome. Every family will be warned to stay far from you, and you may decide, yourself, to stay far from them!"

Lord Montague lifted his chin, his eyes flashing, a small hint of that famous confidence coming back through his voice.

"What is it that you are to offer me?"

A small smile flitted across Lord Foster's face, his eyes narrowing.

"As I have said, there is a chance for a little redemption, perhaps. There is an opportunity here for you to show a little kindness. Knowing that you will be taken to the continent – and this time you certainly *shall* be taken to the continent, for I will make certain to give you a very strong companion for the entirety of the journey – you must now think about your sister."

Lord Montague's eyes flared.

"What do you mean?"

"It is quite simple." Lord Foster gestured to Thomas, who lifted his chin a little more. "Should you choose to cling to Lord Silverton's fortune, then have every assurance that Lady Denfield will join you to take passage to the continent. It will be your responsibility to care for her, of course, but she will be taken with you. There will be no means of escape, for even at present, some of my friends are staying close to her. She has already given you up, however, so mayhap you would think it is fair to punish her in return."

Silence spread across the room for a moment.

"And if I do not?"

Lord Montague had dropped his head and his shoulders were heavy.

"If you wish for your sister to remain in England, then you will return Lord Silverton's fortune to him. I care not whether you have debts, as I well know you have, but you shall not use *his* coin to pay for them."

"In relocating to the continent, you shall free yourself of those debts for a time, I imagine," Thomas remarked, a little dryly. "But I *will* have my fortune again. It was stolen from me. It is to be returned."

Lord Montague lifted his head, his expression ugly.

"My sister will be left with nothing. Penniless. Do you think that a fair offer?"

Thomas caught a sharp look from Lord Thornbridge, seeing his friend lift one eyebrow, and after a moment, he understood what his friend was silently suggesting.

"Lord Montague, you placed a bet that I would wed this Season," he stated, as Lord Montague's eyes narrowed. "I understand that there are a good many gentlemen who have placed bets against you. "Therefore, when your bet is won, the winnings shall go to your sister instead, since you will be abroad." Catching the smile from Lord Thornbridge and the look of surprise from the others, he shrugged both shoulders. "Such a thing will be written in the betting book itself."

Lord Foster blinked, then smiled as Thomas nodded at him.

"But that shall only occur *if* you return Lord Silverton's fortune," Lord Pottinger put in. "To refuse means that both you and Lady Denfield will be on your way to the continent within the week."

Thomas tilted his head, his heart suddenly beating a little more quickly as Lord Montague frowned all the more darkly.

"What shall it be, Montague?" he asked, taking in a long breath. "What is it that you shall decide?"

EPILOGUE

*W*hatever has happened to him?
It felt to Charlotte as though every hour had dragged by with such a slowness that it tore at her, biting at her skin, pulling at her heart. At one point in the day, she had made her way to the large grandfather clock in the hallway, suddenly uncertain as to whether or not it was working, only to see the pendulum swinging and to hear the familiar ticking echoing around her.

Biting on her lip, she made her way to the window to look out at the street below, half praying, half hoping that she would see Lord Silverton's carriage arrive at that very moment – but none came. Her shoulders drooped and she closed her eyes, telling herself that she was being foolish. He had promised to come to call upon her as soon as he could and thus, she had to believe that he would do so.

Taking herself to a chair in the drawing room, she picked up a book that she had left there earlier that morning, found her place, and sat down carefully. The novel had been exceptionally interesting but, at the moment, she struggled to focus on the words. Her eyes flicked to the door at every other moment, her heart quickening at every single sound.

And still, he did not come.

Sighing, Charlotte closed her eyes, closed her book, and rested her head back against the chair. Silently admitting to herself that she was entirely taken up with the gentleman, she let out a long, heavy sigh.

Is this what it is like for one to be in love?

Her eyes flared wide as she half pushed herself out of the chair, blinking furiously. Her emotions were severe, certainly, but was this what one felt when one was in love? Her heart began to quicken all the more as she made her way to the window, one hand pressing to it as she stared out at the view beyond, feeling herself beginning to be filled with an almost inexpressible joy.

A tap at the door had her turning around at once.

"My Lady? Lord Silverton has come to call."

Charlotte's eyes flew immediately to the footman, her heart pounding furiously as she nodded. It was as though his heart had heard the call of hers, and had sent him to her, at the very moment when she had come to realize the true depth of her feelings.

And that flooded her with both joy and an excited nervousness which sent tingling to the very tips of her fingers.

"Yes, of course, send him in. Send him in at once!"

The footman hesitated.

"Lady Landon is not present, and the Earl is engaged in a meeting with gentlemen. I should not like to be the one to risk..." he trailed off and immediately, Charlotte realized his worry.

The man was concerned over the fact that she would be unchaperoned, and if such a thing were to cause any difficulty, then he would certainly lose his position. Quickly, she tossed her head, rising to her feet.

"Send for my maid. And bring Lord Silverton in."

The footman nodded, appearing a little relieved, before disappearing. The maid was better than having no person present at all, and Charlotte could make sure that the door was left ajar also.

She began to pace up and down the room, flexing her fingers as her swirling nervousness grew. She had been waiting eagerly for Lord Silverton's return, but now that he was to join her, she found herself increasingly anxious. What was it that he would say to her? Did he feel the same connection to her as she felt for him? Did he feel the urgency of it, the desire to allow it to grow furiously without being held back? If he did not, then would she find herself left with a broken heart?

The moment that Lord Silverton stepped into the room, however, all anxiety and concern fled. He stepped forward directly, his hands outstretched, and she found herself turning to him, her legs moving of their own accord so that their hands grasped tightly together, his eyes filled with light as he smiled down at her.

"My dear Lady Charlotte," Lord Silverton began quietly. "I do not think that I can ever express my overwhelming gratitude for what you have done."

Hope lifted her spirits higher.

"You have found Lord Montague, then?"

Lord Silverton nodded, the pressure on her hands gently increasing.

"Not only that, but he is in the process of returning my fortune."

Her breath hitched, sending a shiver straight through her.

"So he does have a little humanity in him after all."

At this Lord Silverton shook his head, letting go of one hand so that he might run it through his hair.

"I did not quite believe it myself."

"What made him do such a thing?"

A broken, rueful laugh flew towards her.

"Prepare yourself for a shock, Lady Charlotte... it appears as though Lady Denfield is truly Lord Montague's sister. It was not because of my plight that he felt in any way obliged to help me, but rather because he simply could not allow his sister to be banished with him to the continent. With him returning my fortune, we have ensured that Lady Denfield will have enough money to live a quiet life, where she will not be able to meddle in anybody else's situation. I believe that this circumstance has scared her little, in fact. I expect that she will retreat to the country."

It took Charlotte some moments to accept the fact that Lady Denfield and Lord Montague were truly connected, to the point that she could not speak, such was the surprise. How could it be that she had never known such a thing? The shock of it spread out across her chest, a great and pressing coldness that slowly faded as she looked up at Lord Silverton. He was waiting for her patiently, his eyes smiling down at her as she tilted her face toward him a little more. From that one look, she knew in the depths of her heart that there was something of true significance between them, something that would continue regardless, of whether a calm or a storm was around them.

"I do hope you know, Lord Silverton, that I still would have continued my acquaintance with you, regardless of whether or not you had found your fortune again."

Lord Silverton released her other hand, and for a moment, Charlotte feared that he was to step back, only for his hand to lift so that he might press it lightly to her cheek. His voice was soft when he spoke, sending a tremor straight through her.

"I *do* know that, Charlotte," he answered her quietly. "You have been stalwart through this entire difficulty, refusing to give in, refusing to give up. Even when I was trying to step back from you, you held fast against both my, and your mother's urgings to move away. I do not think that I can express just how much I appreciate that fortitude. If you had not, then I might have found myself betrothed to Lady Denfield – and in the days which would have followed, I would have been shamed beyond recovery." Charlotte swallowed the lump in her throat, hearing just how much affection and appreciation flooded through every word. How dear this gentleman had become to her! His gaze grew a little heavier, fixing itself on her as he lowered his head just a fraction, his voice suddenly dropping low. "I want to assure you, myself, that I never felt a single flicker of emotion for Lady Denfield, I had not even the smallest inkling of affection for her. I appreciated her company, certainly, but that was all there was for her, within my soul." His smile took some of the gravity from his voice. "How could I have been drawn to her when I found that my heart was pulled in an altogether entirely different direction? Pulled towards you, the most wonderful, beautiful, desirable young lady that I have ever had the privilege to set eyes upon."

Before she could say another word, Lord Silverton's head had descended, and his lips were pressed to hers. He had taken a chance in securing a single kiss from her in the hope that she would respond in the same way, and Charlotte could not help but lean into him.

Fully aware that either the maid, or even her father, might

step into the room at any moment, she flung her arms around his neck, pulling herself as close to him as she could, and kissed him back with as much passion as she dared. Lord Silverton's gasp of astonishment at her ardent response was swallowed by her kiss as he wrapped his arms around her waist, her fingers running around the back of his neck, brushing through his hair. It was astonishing, extraordinary, overwhelming, and utterly wonderful, all at the same moment. It was only when a tap came at the door that Charlotte caught her breath, stepping back as Lord Silverton released her at once, even as the maid hurried past them, making her way to the corner of the room and sitting with her face towards the window rather than directly facing Charlotte.

Charlotte giggled as Lord Silverton dropped his head again – but this time, only to talk.

"Forgive me, Charlotte," he murmured, quietly. "I did not know how long we would have alone together, and I did not think I could wait another moment! I must beg your forgiveness if I have been too forward."

Charlotte lifted both hands and pressed them to his face, her thumbs lightly running back across his cheeks.

"You have not been too forward, Lord Silverton," she answered quietly. "I am hopeful that this will lead to something all the more wonderful. My heart belongs to you, for love has lodged itself there and intends to linger there, I fear."

She dropped her hands, but Lord Silverton caught them immediately, his fingers lacing through hers.

"In much the same way as my heart holds fast to you," he told her, making Charlotte's heart lurch, beating furiously at the love she saw in his eyes. "I should tell you, however, that I have every intention of betrothing myself to a *particular* young lady before the Season ends." Laughing at the astonishment in her eyes, he bent down and lightly pressed his lips to hers again for just a moment. "I want very much to make you my own, Lady Charlotte, and I have no intention of delaying, not when I have been kept back from you for so long."

At this, Charlotte found herself filled with such a warmth, such a happiness, and such a light that she could not bear to stay only a few inches away from him. Although the maid was present, she stepped forward and placed herself in Lord Silverton's arms, her head resting on his chest, hearing the steady thrum of his heart as he held her close, his lips brushing the top of her head.

"I do not think that I have ever been as happy as I am at this moment," she whispered softly. "This plan of yours to betroth yourself to a particular young lady... do you have any hope that the lady will say yes?"

With a bright smile, she tipped her head back as Lord Silverton laughed again, brushing his fingers across her cheek and down her neck, sending a flush of tingling down over her skin.

"I suppose that a gentleman can only hope," he told her softly. "Although what would you say, Lady Charlotte, if such a thing should be asked of you?"

Charlotte smiled back into his eyes, finally at peace, her heart filled with love for the gentleman who now held her so tightly in his arms.

"Should you ask, Lord Silverton," she whispered. "Then my answer would be yes."

LOVELY CONCLUSION to the Lost Fortunes series! And at last Lord Montague is vanquished from England and the game of stealing fortunes is over!

If you have missed the first book in the series, a sneak peek is just ahead! A Viscount's Stolen Fortune

Want to try a different series? This one was a bestseller!

Convenient Arrangements: A Regency Romance Collection

MY DEAR READER

Thank you for reading and supporting my books! I hope this story brought you some escape from the real world into the always captivating Regency world. A good story, especially one with a happy ending, just brightens your day and makes you feel good! If you enjoyed the book, would you leave a review on Amazon? Reviews are always appreciated.

Below is a complete list of all my books! Why not click and see if one of them can keep you entertained for a few hours?

The Duke's Daughters Series
The Duke's Daughters: A Sweet Regency Romance Boxset
A Rogue for a Lady
My Restless Earl
Rescued by an Earl
In the Arms of an Earl
The Reluctant Marquess (Prequel)

A Smithfield Market Regency Romance
The Smithfield Market Romances: A Sweet Regency
Romance Boxset
The Rogue's Flower
Saved by the Scoundrel
Mending the Duke
The Baron's Malady

The Returned Lords of Grosvenor Square
The Returned Lords of Grosvenor Square: A Regency
Romance Boxset
The Waiting Bride
The Long Return
The Duke's Saving Grace
A New Home for the Duke

The Spinsters Guild
The Spinsters Guild: A Sweet Regency Romance Boxset
A New Beginning
The Disgraced Bride
A Gentleman's Revenge
A Foolish Wager
A Lord Undone

Convenient Arrangements
Convenient Arrangements: A Regency Romance
Collection
A Broken Betrothal
In Search of Love
Wed in Disgrace
Betrayal and Lies
A Past to Forget
Engaged to a Friend

Landon House
Landon House: A Regency Romance Boxset
Mistaken for a Rake
A Selfish Heart
A Love Unbroken
A Christmas Match
A Most Suitable Bride

An Expectation of Love

Second Chance Regency Romance
Second Chance Regency Romance Boxset
Loving the Scarred Soldier
Second Chance for Love
A Family of her Own
A Spinster No More

Soldiers and Sweethearts
Soldiers and Sweethearts: A Sweet Regency Romance
Boxset
To Trust a Viscount
Whispers of the Heart
Dare to Love a Marquess
Healing the Earl
A Lady's Brave Heart

Ladies on their Own: Governesses and Companions
More Than a Companion
The Hidden Governess
The Companion and the Earl
More than a Governess
Protected by the Companion
A Wager with a Viscount

Lost Fortunes, Found Love
A Viscount's Stolen Fortune
For Richer, For Poorer
Her Heart's Choice
A Dreadful Secret
Their Forgotten Love
His Convenient Match

Christmas Stories

Christmas Kisses (Series)
The Lady's Christmas Kiss
A Viscount's Christmas Queen
Her Christmas Duke

Love and Christmas Wishes: Three Regency Romance
Novellas
A Family for Christmas
Mistletoe Magic: A Regency Romance
Heart, Homes & Holidays: A Sweet Romance Anthology

Happy Reading!

All my love,

Rose

A SNEAK PEEK OF A VISCOUNT'S STOLEN FORTUNE

"What say you, Lord Foster, another round?" William tried to find some sort of inner strength by which he could answer, but there did not appear to be any available to him. "Capital. It is good that you are game."

He blinked furiously, trying to find the words to say that he did not wish to play again, and certainly had not agreed to it. But the words would not come. His jaw seemed tight, unwilling to bend to his will, and anything he wished to say died upon his closed lips.

Closing his eyes, the sounds of cards being dealt reached his ears. Yes, he had drunk a good deal, but he had not imbibed enough to make himself entirely stupid nor stupefied. Why was he struggling to even speak?

"And what shall you bet this time, Lord Foster?"

The gentleman chuckled, and William blinked again, trying to make him out. His vision was a little blurred and for whatever reason, he could not recall the name of the fellow he had sat down to play cards with. This was not his usual gambling den of course - he had come here with some friends, but now was sorely regretting it.

To that end, where were his friends? He did not recall them leaving the table. But then again, he could not remember if any of them had started a game with him, although it would be strange indeed for *all* of them to leave him to play cards alone. Given that this was a part of London none of them were familiar with, however, perhaps it was to be expected. Mayhap they had chosen to play in another gambling house or to enjoy the company of one of the ladies of the night.

My mind seems strangely clear, but I cannot seem to speak.

"If you wish to put everything on the table, then I shall not prevent you."

William shook his head no. The action caused him a little pain and he groaned only to hear the gentleman chuckle.

"Very well. You have a strong constitution, I must say. I do not think that *I* would put down everything on the table. Not if I had already lost so very much. You would be signing over almost your entire fortune to me."

Panic began to spread its way through William's heart. Somebody said something and laughed harshly, leaving the sound to echo through William's mind. He did not want to bet any longer but could not find the strength to speak.

"Shall you look at your cards, Lord Foster?"

William tried to lift a hand towards the cards that he knew were already there, but he could not find them. His fingers struck against the solid wood of the table, but, again, he could not find the cards.

"Goodness, you are a little out of sorts, are you not? Perhaps one too many brandies."

The gentleman's harsh laugh fired William's spirits and he managed to focus on the gentleman's face for a split second. Dark eyes met his gaze and a shock of fair hair pushed back from the gentleman's brow... but then William's vision blurred again.

"I have... I have no wish to bet."

Speaking those words aloud came as a great relief to William. He had managed to say, finally, that he had no wish to continue the game.

"It is a little late, Lord Foster. You cannot pull out of the bet now."

William shook his head, squeezing his eyes closed. He was not entirely sure what game they were playing, but he had no intention of allowing this fellow to take the last bit of his money.

"No." He spoke again, the word hissing from his mouth, as though it took every bit of strength that he had to speak it. "No, I end this bet."

Somehow, he managed to push himself to his feet. A strong hand gripped his arm and William had no strength to shake it off. Everything was swirling. The room threatened to tilt itself from one side to the next, but he clung to whoever it was that held his arm. He had no intention of letting himself fall. Nausea roiled in his stomach, and he took in great breaths, swallowing hard so that he would not cast up his accounts.

"No, I make no bet. I withdraw it."

"You are not being a gentleman." The man's voice had turned hard. "A gentleman does not leave the table in such circumstances – given that I am a Viscount and you one also, it is honorable to finish the game. Perhaps you just need another brandy. It would calm your nerves."

William shook his head. That was the last thing he required.

"Gentlemen or no, I will not be continuing with this bet. I will take what I have remaining and depart." It was as if the effects of the brandy were wearing off. He could speak a little more clearly and stand now without difficulty as he let go of the other man's arm. His vision, however, remained blurry. "I will gather up the last of my things and be on my way. My friends must be nearby."

"You will sit down, and you will finish the game."

William took in a long breath - not to raise his courage, but rather to muster his strength. He wanted to *physically* leave this gambling house for good.

"I shall not." His voice shook with the effort of speaking loudly and standing without aid. "I fully intend to leave this gambling house at once, with all that I have remaining."

Whilst his resolve remained strong, William could not account for the blow that struck him on the back of the head. Evidently, his determination to leave had displeased the gentleman and darkness soon took William. His coin remained on the table and as he sank into the shadows, he could not help but fear as to what would become of it.

CHAPTER ONE

"My Lord." The gentle voice of his butler prodded William from sleep. Groaning, he turned over and buried his face in the pillow. "My Lord." Again, came the butler's voice, like an insistent prodding that jerked William into wakefulness. The moment he opened his eyes, everything screamed. "I must apologize for my insistence, but five of your closest acquaintances are in the drawing room, determined to speak with you. Lord Stoneleigh is in a somewhat injured state."

"Injured?" Keeping his eyes closed, William flung one hand over them as he turned over. "What do you mean?"

The butler cleared his throat gently.

"I believe that he has been stabbed, my Lord." The butler's voice remained calm, but his words blunt. "A surgeon has already seen to him, but his arm may be damaged permanently, I was told."

"Permanently?" The shock that flooded through William forced his eyes open as he pushed himself up on his elbows. "Are you quite certain?"

"Yes, my Lord. I did, of course, inquire whether there

was anything the gentleman needed, but he stated that the only thing required was for him to speak with you."

"And he is well?"

The butler blinked.

"As well as can be expected, my Lord."

William nodded slowly, but then wished he had not, given the pain in his head.

"Must it be at this very moment?" he moaned, as the butler looked at him, the dipping of his mouth appearing a little unsympathetic. "I do not wish to appear heartless but my head..." Squeezing his eyes closed, he let out a heavy sigh. "Can they not wait until I am a little recovered?"

The butler shook his head.

"I apologize, my Lord, but I was told that they wish to speak to you urgently and that they would not leave until they had spoken with you. That is why I came to you at once. It appears most severe indeed."

"I see." William realized that he had no other choice but to rise, pushing one hand through his hair as the pain in his head grew. "This is most extraordinary. Whatever is it that they wish to speak to me about so urgently?"

"I could not say, my Lord." The butler stood dutifully back as William tried to rise from his bed. "Your valet is waiting outside the door; shall I fetch him?"

"Yes." William's head was pounding, and he grimaced as he attempted to remove his legs from the sheets. They appeared to be tangled in them, and it took him some time to extricate himself, hampered entirely by the pain in his head. "I am sure that, after last night, my friends must also be feeling the effects of a little too much enjoyment," he muttered aloud. "Why then-"

Shock tore through him as he suddenly realized that he could not recall what had happened the previous evening.

He could not even remember how he had made his way home. A heaviness dropped into the pit of his stomach, although there was no explanation for why he felt such a thing. Had something happened last night that he had forgotten about?

"Jefferies." Moving forward so that his valet could help him dress, William glanced at his butler who had been on his way out the door. "You may speak freely. Was I in something of a sorry state when I returned home last evening?"

There was no flicker of a smile in the butler's eyes. His expression remained entirely impassive.

"No, my Lord, you were not in your cups. You were entirely unconscious."

William blinked rapidly.

"Unconscious?"

The butler nodded.

"Yes, my Lord."

"Are you quite sure?"

The butler lifted one eyebrow.

"Yes, my Lord. The carriage arrived, but no one emerged. Your coachman and I made certain that you were safe in your bed very soon afterward, however."

Confusion marred William's brow. It was most unlike him to drink so very much that he became lost in drunkenness. He could not recall the last time he had done so. A little merry, perhaps, but never to the point of entirely losing his consciousness.

How very strange.

Shoving his fingers through his short, dark hair in an attempt to soothe the ache, William winced suddenly as his fingers found a rather large bump on the side of his head. Wincing, he traced it gingerly.

That certainly was not there yesterday.

It seemed that the pain in his head was not from drinking a little too much, but rather from whatever had collided with his head. A little concerned that he had been involved in some sort of fight – again, entirely out of character for him – he now wondered if his friends were present to make certain that he was either quite well or willing to take on whatever consequences now faced him. William urged his valet to hurry. *Did not my butler say that Lord Stoneleigh was injured? Surely, I could not have been the one to do such a thing as that!*

"I am glad to see you a little recovered, my Lord." The butler's voice remained a dull monotone. "Should I bring you something to drink? Refreshments were offered to your acquaintances, but they were refused."

"Coffee, please."

The pain in his head was lingering still, in all its strength, but William ignored it. A new sense of urgency settled over him as he hurried from his bedchamber and made his way directly to the drawing room. Conversation was already taking place as he stepped inside, only to stop dead as he entered the room. His five acquaintances, whom he had stepped out with the previous evening, all turned to look at him as one. Fear began to tie itself around William's heart.

"Lord Stoneleigh." William put out one hand towards his friend. "You are injured, my butler tells me."

His friend nodded but his eyes remained a little wide.

"I am, but that is not the reason we are here. We must know if you are in the same situation as we all find ourselves at present?"

The question made very little sense to William, and he took a moment to study Lord Stoneleigh before turning to the rest of his friends.

"The same situation?" he repeated. "Forgive me, I do not understand."

"We should never have set foot in that seedy place." Lord Thornbridge pushed one hand through his hair, adding to its disarray. Silently, William considered that it appeared as though Lord Thornbridge had been doing such a thing for many hours. "It was I who became aware of it first. I spoke to the others, and they are all in the same situation. You are the only one we have not yet spoken to."

"I do not understand what you mean." More confused than ever, William spread his hands. "What situation is it that you speak of?"

It was Lord Wiltsham who spoke first. Every other gentleman was staring at William as though they had some dreadful news to impart but did not quite know how to say it.

"My friend, we have lost our fortunes."

Shock poured into William's heart. He stared back at Lord Wiltsham uncomprehendingly.

"Your fortunes?"

"Yes. Some more, some less but a good deal of wealth is gone from us all."

William closed his eyes, his chest tight. How could this be?

"He does not know." William's eyes flew open, swinging towards Lord Pottinger as he looked at the others. "He cannot tell us either."

"Tell you?" William's voice was hoarse. "What is it that you mean? How can you have lost your fortunes? What is it you were expecting to hear from me?"

He stared at one gentleman, then moved his gaze to the next. These gentlemen were his friends, and how they could have lost so much coin in one evening was incomprehensible to him. They were not foolish gentlemen. Yes, they enjoyed cards and gambling and the like on occasion, but they would never have been so lacking in wisdom, regardless of how much they had imbibed.

"Some of us do not wish to say it, but it is true." Lord Silverton glanced at William, then looked away. "We have realized that our fortunes have been lost. Some have a little more left than others, but we are now in great difficulty."

William shook his head.

"It cannot be. You are all gentlemen with wisdom running through you. You would not behave so without consideration! I cannot believe that you have all willingly set your coin into the hands of others. You would not do such a thing to your family name."

Lord Stoneleigh was the next to speak.

"I fear you may also be in the same situation, my friend." His eyes were dull, his face pale – although mayhap that came from his injury. "You are correct that we are gentlemen of wisdom, but making our way to that part of London last evening was not wise. It appears that certain gentlemen - or those masquerading as gentlemen - have taken our coin from us in ways that are both unscrupulous and unfair."

Fire tore through William as he again shook his head.

"I would never give away my fortune to the point of poverty," he declared determinedly. "I am certain I would not have done so."

"As we thought also." Lord Pottinger threw up his hands. "But you find us now without fortune, leaving us struggling for the remainder of our days. That is, unless we can find a way to recover it from those unscrupulous sorts who have taken it from us... although how we are to prove that they have done so is quite beyond me."

William took a deep breath. He was quite certain that he would never have behaved in such a foolish way as was being suggested, but the fear that lingered in his friend's eyes was enough to unsettle him. If it was as they said, then he might well discover himself to be in the same situation as they.

"I am quite sure that I cannot..." Trailing off at the heaviness in each of his friend's eyes, William sighed, nodded, and rose to his feet. "I will have my man of business discover the truth," he declared, as his friends glanced at each other. "It *cannot* be as you say. I would certainly never..."

A sudden gasp broke from his lips as the memories began to pour into his mind. He recalled why the pain in his head was so severe, remembered the gentleman who had insisted upon him betting, even though William had been somehow unable to speak. A memory of attempting to declare that he would not bet anymore forced its way into his mind – as well as the pain in his head which had come swiftly thereafter.

"You remember now, I think." Lord Wiltsham's smile was rueful. "Something happened, did it not?"

William began to nod slowly, his heart pounding furiously in his chest.

"It is as I feared." Lord Wiltsham sighed and looked away. "We have all been taken in by someone. I do not know who, for it appears to be different for each of us. Going to that east part of London – to those 'copper hells' instead of our own gambling houses - has made a difficult path for all of us now. We have very little fortune left to speak of."

"But I did not wish to gamble." Hearing his voice hoarse, William closed his eyes. Thoughts were pouring into his mind, but he could make very little sense of them. "I told him I did not wish to gamble."

"Then perhaps you did not." A faint note of hope entered Lord Wiltsham's voice. "Mayhap you remain free of this injury."

William opened his eyes and looked straight at his friend.

"No, I do not believe I am." The truth brought fresh pain to his heart. "I remember now that someone injured me. I do not recall anything after that, but my butler informs me that I arrived home in an unconscious state. If it is as you say, then I am sure that whoever I was playing cards with made certain that they stole a great deal of coin. Lifting his hand, he pinched the bridge of his nose. "Perhaps I have lost everything."

"I will be blunt with you, my friend." Lord Thornbridge's eyes were clear, but his words brought fear. "It sounds as though you will discover that you *have* lost a great deal. It may not be everything, but it will certainly be enough to change the course of your life from this day forward."

The frankness with which he spoke was difficult for William to hear. He wanted to awaken all over again, to imagine that this day was not as it seemed.

"We ought never to have left our usual haunts." Lord Pottinger dropped his face into his hands, his words muffled. "In doing so, we appear to have been taken advantage of by those who pretended to be naught but gentlemen."

"They have done more than take advantage." William's voice was hoarse. "I recall that I did not feel well last night. My vision was blurred, and I do not even remember the gentleman's face. And yet somehow, I have managed to lose my fortune to him. My behavior does not make sense, and nor does any of yours." Silence filled the room as he stretched his hands out wide, looking at each one in turn.

Lord Thornbridge was the first to speak in response.

"You believe that this was deliberate. You think that these... scoundrels... gave us something to make us lose our senses?"

"In my case, I am certain that they did." William bit his lip. "I cannot give you a clear explanation for it, but I am quite certain that I would never have behaved in such a manner. The responsibility of the title has been heavy on my shoulders for many years, and I would never have given such a fortune away."

"Nor would I. But yet it seems that I have done so." Lord Pottinger shook his head. "I cannot see any recourse."

"And yet it is there." William took a step closer, refusing to give in to the dread which threatened to tear away every single shred of determination that tried to enter his heart. "The only way we will regain our fortune is to find those responsible, and demand that they return our coin to us. I will not stand by and allow myself to lose what should see me through the remainder of my days – and to set my heir in good standing!"

His friends did not immediately reply. None answered with hope nor expectation, for they all shook their heads and looked away as though they were quite lost in fear and darkness. William could feel it clutching at him also, but he refused to allow its spindly fingers to tighten around his neck.

"We have each lost our fortune in different ways." Lord Thornbridge shrugged, then dropped his shoulders. "However are we supposed to find those responsible, when we were all in differing situations?"

William spread his hands.

"I cannot say as yet, but there must be something that each of us can do to find out who is to blame. Otherwise, the future of our lives remains rather bleak."

A sudden thought of Lady Florence filled his mind. He had been about to ask for her hand, but should he tell her about what had occurred, then William was quite certain that she would refuse him. After all, no young lady would consider a gentleman who had no fortune.

His heart sank.

"You are right." Lord Wiltsham's voice had a tad more confidence and William lifted his head. "We cannot sit here and simply accept that our fortunes are gone, not if we believe that they have been unfairly taken. Instead, we must do all we can to find the truth and to recover whatever coin we can."

"I agree." Lord Stoneleigh tried to spread his hands, then winced with the pain from his injury. "I simply do not know how to go about it."

"That will take some time, and I would suggest that you give yourself a few days to recover from the shock and to think about what must be done." Lord Thornbridge now also appeared to be willing to follow William's lead. "Since I have very little coin left, I must make changes to my household immediately – and I shall have to return to my estate to do it. Thereafter, however, I will consider what I shall do to find out where my fortune has gone. Perhaps we can encourage each other, sharing any news about what we have discovered with each other."

"Yes, I quite agree." Letting out a slow breath, William considered what he would now face. It would be difficult, certainly, yet he was prepared. He knew how society would treat him once news about his lack of funds was discovered and William would have to find the mental strength to face it. What was important to him at present was that he found the perpetrators, for that was the only way he could see to regain some of his fortune – and his standing in society.

"I should speak to my man of business at once." William dropped his head and blew out a huff of breath before he lifted it again. "This will not be a pleasant time, gentlemen. But at least we have the companionship and encouragement of each other as we face this dreadful circumstance together."

His friends nodded, but no one smiled. A heavy sense of gloom penetrated the air and William's heart threatened to sink lower still as he fought to cling to his hope that he would restore his fortune soon enough.

I will find out who did this. And I shall not remain in their grip for long.

CHECK out the rest of the story in the Kindle store A Viscount's Stolen Fortune

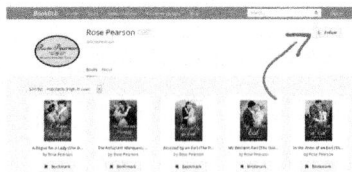

Printed in Great Britain
by Amazon